PARADISE VALLEY FEUD

by

Paul K. McAfee

Dales Large Print Books
Long Preston, North Yorkshire,
BD23 4ND, England.

British Library Cataloguing in Publication Data.

McAfee, Paul K.
    Paradise Valley feud.

A catalogue record of this book is
available from the British Library

ISBN   1-84262-053-3 pbk

First published in Great Britain 2000 by Robert Hale Ltd.

Copyright © Paul K. McAfee 2000

Cover illustration © Faba by arrangement with
Norma Editorial S. A.

The right of Paul K. McAfee to be identified as the author of this
work has been asserted by him in accordance with the
Copyright, Designs and Patents Act, 1988

Published in Large Print 2001 by arrangement with
Robert Hale Ltd.

Dales Large Print is an imprint of Library Magna Books Ltd.

Printed and bound in Great Britain by
T.J. (International) Ltd., Cornwall, PL28 8RW

Dedicated with love
to the memory of my brothers,
Carl, Russell and Oscar

ONE

Luke Kane looked down from the shelf overlooking the valley he had discovered so long ago, which had become the home of himself, Hannah, and now eight-year-old John Lucus Kane, their son, born in Paradise Valley. Kane's heart warmed as he thought of his son whom he had left sleeping while he came here to look over his ranch once again.

It was ten years since he had found this pristine valley, beautiful in its innocence and abounding with all anyone would need to make a home for himself and his family. Teeming with animal life, meadows lush with rich grasses and foliage for cattle and horses. Down there, just above the creek on a small knoll, surrounded by huge water-oak trees, was their home. Built to become part of the land, made from the trees of the valley, it had been created by his and Hannah's hands. Its rooms were spacious and inviting, with high pitched ceilings, large and open. Two huge fireplaces, created with stones from the fields, lifted above the ends of the main part of the house. There were four bedrooms, one turned into Kane's ranch office, the others for family and guests. The kitchen was spacious, with one of the fireplaces, plus a cast-iron range, brought from the territorial capital at much cost and effort. The room was open and light, with many shelves and closets for food materials and other needs for the cook. The final addition to the house had come late, but consisted of a full wrap-around porch, with eaves covered with the same shades of the house, inviting and cool with breezes coming up the valley, hand-wrought chairs, benches and stools invited the weary traveller.

Luke Kane sighed. This was his and Hannah's. And one day it would all belong to John Lucus. At the moment it was nothing but pure pleasure for him to look down over the valley and see what he and his strong wife had created themselves, with the aid of One Foot, a crippled Crow Indian who had found his way into the valley. Later the Indian had appeared with two younger men, with young wives, offering to work for him for food and for the privilege of living in the valley.

Kane welcomed their help and soon the four of them, along with Hannah and the young wives, were into a pattern of work that moved the ranch along toward becoming what Kane dreamed of having. A horse ranch, with well-bred animals, and a small herd of cattle of choice breed for food and for sale for cash money to bring in those things that could not be made by their own hands. The Indians made their lodges close to the cliff, several hundred yards from the narrow crevice which was still the entrance to the valley, found ten years past by Kane.

He saw the sun coming over the rim of the mountains to the east, pushing away the dawn and flooding the valley with warm light. Day was here and Hannah was on the porch tapping an iron triangle calling him in to breakfast.

Kane was in the tack shed working on a saddle, when John Lucus came scampering up the path from the house.

'Pa,' he shouted. 'Someone's coming ... a stranger!'

Luke placed the saddle on a rack and joined his son in the yard in front of the barn and the several small sheds nearby. He looked up the slope toward the shelf on to which the entrance to the valley opened. A horseman was making his way down the slope toward the ranch house. Eyeing him closely Luke seemed to recognize him, but could not put a name to him. A vague memory stirred as the man drew closer and finally pulled up at the edge of the barn yard.

'Kane? Luke Kane?' the man asked in a raspy voice. John Lucus came close to Luke and wrapped his arms about his leg.

'Who's he?' he asked his father in a small voice. Somehow, even in his tender years, he seemed to recognize impeding danger.

'I don't know, Johnnie. Get back now.' He took the boy's arms from around him and pushed him away. 'Go to the house.' His son slowly, reluctantly backed away several feet, but did not leave the barnyard.

'Yeah, I'm Luke Kane. But I don't know you,' Luke answered the rider who was slowly dismounting and turning to face him. Luke frowned. Western curtesy was that one did not dismount as such unless invited to do so. This visitor was not following that rule of society. He faced Luke defiantly.

'No, of course you wouldn't recognize me. It's been over ten years, and besides you

10

wouldn't care.' His eyes narrowed and glittered in a sudden surge of emotion.

'Over ten years ago you killed my brothers and turned me over to the law. I spent those years in the territorial prison and I remembered your face every moment I was there. I'm Henry Rawlins.'

Luke remembered. He recalled the startled look on the face of a young man, still mostly boy, when his bullet slammed into him and drove life from his body. The boy had come at him with a drawn Bowie knife, giving him nothing to do but to stop him. The wound was instantly fatal, and Luke never forgave himself for the shooting. He left the Texas Rangers because of the incident and wore no sidearm for several years until an occasion arose which once again called for his expertise with the gun.

He nodded to the man. 'I remember. I have been sorry all my life that I had to shoot your brother. But he gave me no quarter – and he was involved in cattle-rustling.'

Henry Rawlins shook his head. 'No matter now,' he said softly. 'I swore revenge against you and now is the time.'

Luke spread his arms. 'Killing me won't bring you peace of mind, Rawlins.' He spread his arms widely from his body. 'I'm not armed.'

Rawlins shook his head. 'No matter,' he said. 'I'd back shoot you just as quick as look at you while I done it.' Luke steeled himself and tensed to throw himself to the ground when he saw Rawlins reach for his sidearm, a .45 caliber revolver.

There was a *swish* and a humming noise. Rawlins' pistol was half out of his holster when an arrow pierced his back, plowing through his heart and protruding two inches from the chest wall. He yelled in agony and, dropping the six-gun back into the leather, he looked up at Luke. Blood spilled from his mouth and down his chin, then, hands still tugging at the arrow-head, he lurched one step and fell forward into the dirt of the barnyard.

Shaken at the narrow escape, Kane looked at the shed against which One Foot the Crow Indian stood with an Indian war bow in his hand. Two other arrows were thrust into his belt. The Indian grunted.

'You have bad enemies, Luke Kane,' he said. 'You unarmed, so I evened up the fight some, huh?'

Luke nodded and grimaced ruefully. 'I *had* an enemy, all right. And if you hadn't taken

12

a hand, I'd be dead meat. Obliged, my friend.'

One Foot grunted again and nodded. 'I have my nephews take him away, if you want. No one need know he here.'

Luke was thoughtful a long minute. He looked at the dead man. He raised his eyes and saw that John Lucus had gone to his mother and stood in the doorway with her, his eyes large in his pale face. Hannah looked at Luke and nodded slightly.

'We are all right, Luke. You do what you think best. But remember that Clarence Holland is sheriff of Red Rock. He might know that this man was coming here. Maybe you should at least let him know what happened.'

Luke eyed her, his eyes soft. What a woman! She had worked like a field-hand with him getting this ranch on the way. Now, she had seen a man die in front of her, and still stood there, understanding just what the situation called for. He nodded.

'I'll make a trip into Red Rock in a few days and let Holland know what happened here. He may have a flyer on Rawlins. I think he went up for life, without parole. If so, he was an escaped prisoner.' He motioned to One Foot. 'You and your nephews take him away. You can have his weapons and whatever you can use out of his possibles. And the horse is yours if you want it. If not turn it loose. It'll join my herd in a little while.' The Indian nodded shortly.

'We do,' he grunted. Kane left the barnyard and went into the house. He was shaken from several directions. He did not like that the man had found him so easily. Someone who knew the location of the entrance to the valley had to have informed him and given directions. Who that might have been, he could not know. Also, and certainly not secondary, the narrow escape from death, leaving Hannah and John Lucus and all this they had worked for because of a family vendetta. He grimly determined never again to leave the house unarmed.

Red Rock looked much the same as when he and Hannah had left it. Leaving at midnight, with few possessions in blanket rolls, fleeing through the Lazy L ranch of his friend Rube Lincoln, and on through the Blue Mesa to this hidden valley the entrance to which only he knew, he had been back here to this small high plains town only a few times, coming in quietly and quickly taking care of business and buying those

14

staples needed beyond what they produced themselves. He knew the sheriff well, and had spoken to him briefly whenever he had come here. Now he had a different reason to find Clarence Holland, the present lawman of this part of the territory.

He pulled up before the sheriff's office, and dismounted, wrapped the reins about the hitch rail and stepped on to the boardwalk, just as the sheriff opened the door of his office and paused, looking at him.

'Luke Kane ... I ain't seen you for a coon's age. How are you?' He came forward with an outstretched hand. 'I'm glad you come in. I want to talk to you about something what might concern you and Hannah.'

They shook hands and went into the office. 'Pull up a chair,' Holland said. 'I just happen to have a pint of Kentucky Bourbon I bluffed a liquor salesman out of. How about a taste of that?'

Luke grinned. 'You just yanked my chain, Clarence.' The sheriff produced the bottle and poured a drink in two glasses. They sat and sipped the drink and exchanged casual talk for several minutes. Finally Luke sat his glass down and looked at the sheriff.

'Clarence, there's been a man killed on my ranch.'

Holland eyed him thoughtfully. 'Tell me about it,' he said.

'He appeared in my barnyard about three days ago,' Luke told him. 'A man from out of my past, named Henry or Hank Rawlins. He was one of three brothers I caught stealing high-bred beef, when I was in the Texas Rangers. Two of them drawed on me and I killed them. This one was on guard and I slipped up and got him without gunplay and he went to prison for cattle-thieving. Now, it seems he's out and I suppose the first thing he thought of was to get even with me for gunning down his brothers.'

Clarence eyed him closely. 'Was this the occasion when one of them you shot was a kid, still in his teens? You told me about something like that.'

Luke nodded. 'The Rawlins brothers, yes. Henry somehow found out how to get into my valley ranch and appeared, geared for a gunfight. He walked up on me when I was unarmed. He started to gun me down, regardless I was clean. The old Indian, One Foot, working for the ranch, stepped around the corner of a shed and sent an arrow through him, back to front, just when his gun was half out of the leather. That old

Crow saved my life.' He eyed the sheriff intently. 'We buried Rawlins and I come in to tell you about it.'

The sheriff looked at his desk for a few long moments, then, without speaking, reached into a drawer and pulled out a thick folder of papers. He opened it and began to search through his collection of flyers, seeking individuals who were wanted by the law. After several discards, he grunted and picked one out of the folder. He handed it to Luke.

'Henry Rawlins killed a guard in the prison and with four others escaped. All of them have been caught or killed when approached by a lawman to surrender. All but Rawlins. He's wanted for prison escape, for murder when he robbed a small bank in Laramie. Actually, you saved the territorial government money by taking him out of the picture.'

Luke nodded and leaned back in the chair. He took a sack of Bull Durham from his jacket pocket and rolled a cigarette, lighting it from a wooden match. Drawing the smoke deeply into his lungs and letting it out slowly, he nodded again.

'Thanks, Clarence. I'll leave the rest of what has to be done up to you.' He took his hat and rose to leave. The sheriff waved him back to his chair.

'There's something you should know,' he said.

Kane looked at him questioningly and settled back into the chair. 'What would that be?' he asked.

'Josh Carter is back in the territory,' he said. 'And he ain't running with a very good bunch of friends.'

Kane lowered his head. The sheriff's information had disturbed him. Josh Carter was the cousin of the former sheriff, Bruce Carter. That individual had been Hannah's former husband, but had lost his life by a strange and terrible accident at the entrance to Luke's valley. Why was Josh Carter back, and according to the sheriff, running with a bad bunch of men? He shook his head.

'Josh left here with some people accusing him of cattle-rustling,' he said, looking at the sheriff. 'Why would he come back here, knowing that?'

'It's been ten years, Luke, since that happened. He may believe it is forgotten, or can put out the word that he has changed his ways. Who knows? I wanted you to know so you can be ready if he should front you about something. After all, you gave him a pretty good thump a time or two. Maybe that made him think.'

Luke rose again. 'I don't think so. But thanks for the information.' He put his hat on. 'I have a few things to pick up at the mercantile, and then I'll be heading out.'

The sheriff went to the door with him. They shook hands and Luke turned down the boardwalk towards the mercantile.

George Holt, owner of the mercantile, looked up as Luke came through the door. His face lighted up as he saw who it was, and he came around the counter where he was standing with out-thrust hand. 'Luke Kane, by golly. It sure is good to see you.'

'Everyone is fine, George. Hannah sent her regards and John Lucus said he wanted some of that peppermint stick candy, if you had any.'

George laughed. 'I keep it just for him.'

They used up several minutes conversing and then Kane ordered those articles Hannah had suggested.

'I'll be around in a little while and pick them up,' Luke said. 'Right now I'm gonna visit Charles Bridges's barbershop and see if he has a haircut that will fit me.'

Kane stepped from the mercantile on to the boardwalk and turned towards the barbershop, to come face to face with a stranger. The man eyed him narrowly, crowding the walk, intentionally blocking his way. In the street back of him were two others, dressed in range clothes, and each carrying a six-gun on the right hip, slung low. The man before him also carried the sidearm, its worn black butt gleaming dully from the leather.

'You're Kane?' the man asked.

Luke eyed him calmly, taking in the beard, the glinting mean eye, and the stance with the right hand hooked in the belt above the six-gun.

Luke nodded. 'I'm Kane,' he said shortly.

'Wa'al, you don't look to be the he-wolf I've been told you was. No matter. Come on down frum the walk an' you an' me are gonna take a leetle waltz of our own. I got a friend who told me to bounce you around some if I saw you, an' a man down the street pointed you out as you come into the store.'

Kane shook his head. 'I'm not fighting you, stranger. You mean nothing to me. And whoever put you on to me, had me wrong. Now, let's go about our own ways and forget any fighting.' He moved to step around the man, but the stranger moved and blocked him again.

'Coward, huh? I was told you was a ring-tailed-bobcat mixed with a bull-dog, when it come to fightin'. But I guess I was told wrong. Wa'al, how about this...'

The man made a move, reaching toward his gun belt.

'Take your hand away from the gun, mister. There's no gunplay in my town unless I do it myself.'

Clarence Holland, the sheriff, had come up behind the group.

The man facing Kane turned and saw the badge on the sheriffs vest. 'This rangy an' me has some business to finish–'

'Shuck your gun,' Luke said softly. 'You called me a coward. No one calls me that and gets away with it. Someone sent you to bounce me around, you said. Well, this is your chance.' He unbuckled his gun belt and laid it on the porch behind him. He stepped into the street, and looked at the man who had insisted on the fight. 'Well?'

'Wa'al now, this is better. My name's Buck Leonard an' I'm here to whup you good an' then leave you a message.' He removed his gun belt and stepped into the street.

Clarence Holland spoke up. 'Ya'll hold up a minute.' He glanced up as George Holt stepped from the store, holding a huge, single-barrelled, sawed-off, 12 gauge Greener shotgun.

'I remember something about you, Leonard, if that's your name. Seems that I recall readin' that you always carried a hide-out gun or knife. Are you sure you're completely unarmed right now?'

'Course I am,' Buck snarled. 'Right thar's my pistol to prove it.' He pointed to his weapons at the sheriff's feet.

George Holt waggled the Greener at the other two men. 'Get yourselves back against the wall of the building and drop your guns, too.' The couple did as the stern-faced store owner ordered. 'Now, truthfully, knowing Buck here as you do, is he unarmed? Or does he have a hidden weapon on him yet that you know about?' Both men shook their heads. George eared back the shotgun, the click of the hammer sounding ominously. He leveled the gun at the two men.

'Now, you know how this cannon works. It's sawed off, and will scatter purty good. I might shoot at one of you for lying to me, and get the other one, too–'

'Here, now! Just wait one damn minute!' One of the men against the building blurted out. 'Hold up on that bufferlo gun! I ain't afeered of nothin' in life, but a mad grizzly bear-sow who's got her cubs, or one of them Greeners. I ain't gonna get my hide made into a sieve fer Buck ner nobody else. Sheriff, he's got a pig-sticker hid thar in his right boot.'

The sheriff drew his gun, cocking it as it came level and pointed it at Buck's midriff. 'You've got thirty seconds to get that knife out an' over here by your pistol. Do it!'

Buck scowled at his companion who had spoken up. Cursing, he reached into the top of his right boot and slowly withdrew an eight-inch hunting knife. He grunted and tossed it to where the gun belt and pistol lay, and straightened. 'Now, can we get on with this dance?'

Holland looked at the man who had indicated Buck had a knife hidden. 'Any more pretties you can think of that he might have stuck away?'

The man shook his head. 'Not as I know of, Sheriff.'

Holland looked at Kane. 'I ain't right pleased this is goin' on,' he said. 'But if it has to be, cut the tiger loose.'

Buck was looking at Holland as the sheriff spoke. He threw himself at Kane and whipped a huge fist at his jaw. Luke was expecting some such maneuver and ducked the big man, slamming him in the kidneys as he lurched by. Buck yelled in pain at the blow, and whirling, rushed Kane, lowering his head to butt him in the stomach. Again Luke anticipated his movement and slipped by him. As he slid to a stop and turned, Kane slammed a rock-hard fist into his face. Buck's nose was broken and blood spurted down his face and chest. Cursing he rushed Kane and they stood face to face and traded blows that hurt each of them.

Buck was big. More than six feet tall, and weighing around two hundred twenty pounds. At one time he had been all muscle and bones, but fat from careless living, too much whiskey and beer, along with other habits had left him softer than he appeared to be. Kane soon realized this and quickly took advantage. He slammed rights and lefts into the man's belly, shifted to the sides, where a roll of fat made itself easily seen. Buck was getting short of breath. His eyes narrowed, for he had not been bested in a street fight since he was in his teens. A bully by nature, he expected his opponents to be wary of his size, that they would give way to his first bull-like rushes.

But this Luke Kane, whom he had judged to be an easy adversary, was turning out to be something else. He had been warned that Kane was not an easy pick, and that he seldom gave an inch, even when he was losing. But Buck tossed this off as talk, and had entered the struggle fully expecting to see Kane stretched out on the ground by this time. But, rather, he himself was losing wind, and had found the fists of Kane to be everywhere – in the belly, in the heart area, in the face, and he suddenly knew that here was an adversary most likely to best him. With this thought he drew a deep breath and launched himself headlong at Kane, his rush and bulk driving the rancher back several steps.

Kane was tiring. He knew the weight and reach of the man was greater than his own, and it was taking its toll. Buck's huge fists had landed again and again during their toe to toe flurry, and Kane felt their impact to his very bones. Back pedaling from Buck, he drew his breath deeply and as the big man came at him, set himself and met him with blows carrying all the strength of arms and shoulders. He directed his blows to the belly of the man, shifting quickly to the neck and face, searching for the point on the rock-hard jaw that would drive him back. One of his fists slammed into Buck's jaw just in front of his ear. Buck's eyes blared and he stepped backwards, shaking his head.

Luke bore in and, moving quickly and with deliberate aim, slammed connecting blows to the face and jaw of the man again and again. Buck stumbled and Kane reached in and with all the weight of his body and strength of arms and shoulders, crushed through his defense. Buck's chin snapped sideways and his eyes rolled. He fell, out on his feet.

Kane leaned over Buck's inert form, gasping for breath. Seeing his enemy unconscious he staggered to the horse trough across the street and thrust his head into the water, coming up shaking his head and sitting down abruptly on one end of the trough.

The sheriff walked over to him. 'You all right, Luke?'

Luke nodded. 'Except I feel like a log wagon rolled over me a couple of times, I'm fine.' He looked over at Buck Leonard. 'Hold him a couple of days, will you? See if you get out of him the name of whoever set him on to me.'

The sheriff shook his head. 'Won't have to. George Holt stuck that old Greener of his nearly up one of them boys' nose, an' he told just who it was.'

Luke pushed wet hair back out of his eyes and looked up at the sheriff. 'Who was it?'

Holland grimaced and then shrugged.

'It was Josh Carter,' he said.

TWO

The two men with Buck Leonard talked finally, long and loud, when they realized their choice was meager, either prison with no parole, or talk and walk out of Red Rock and never show their faces there again. As they sat in the sheriff's office and made their confessions, Buck Leonard gained consciousness and yelled and cursed them for being yellow-livered cowards, and that when he got out, he would find them and kill them both.

'Never you mind him,' Sheriff Holland said. 'When we're through with him he won't even think about chasin' you down. Now, take your gear, climb on to your hosses an' don't let me see either of you again.'

The two took no time following the

sheriffs instructions. As Luke and the sheriff heard the beat of hooves fading as the two men raced their mounts beyond the town limits, Luke looked at Holland.

'Suppose they'll high-tail it to Josh Carter and give him a rundown on what happened here?'

The sheriff shrugged. 'Maybe so, maybe not. I don't think that ranny in there and the ones who sided him were too much on the buddy-buddy side.' He shook his head. 'No, I think they're out of the picture now. I doubt very much if we'll see them around here again soon, if ever.'

Josh Carter was angry. Word had gotten back to him that Luke Kane had beaten Buck Leonard in his attempt to follow Josh's orders to do as much bodily harm to him as possible, without killing him. *That* Carter wanted to do himself at the appropriate moment.

Carter had located Kane's valley several months ago, when a wandering member of the owl-hoot trails became wordy in a saloon, and after a half-bottle of skull-blasting liquor, had disclosed that he had seen a place that was almost a paradise, if there was such a thing in this world. It was not long until Josh, at the table with him over a dilatory game of five-card stud, drew the story out of him.

When the drunk had finally dropped his head upon the table, overcome by the liquor, Josh had the picture of a beautiful valley, uninhabited except for one man and his wife and a kid. There were two or three Indians working on the spread, which took in the entire valley. Ten miles of high meadows, stands of good timber, plenty of water and, so far as the men could tell, no other inhabitants for miles around. He was proving up a ranch of some hundred thousand acres, with wild horses to catch and tame and sell, and plenty of room for a nice herd of beef.

'How did you get into this paradise?' Josh asked the man.

'Thar's an old Injun trail at the far end of the valley,' he said. 'It ain't been used in a hundred years I suspect. Its rough and high and narrow, but I got over it on my hoss an' camped there a couple of weeks dodgin' a bounty hunter.'

Suddenly Josh knew, without doubt, that this was the valley Luke Kane had disappeared into occasionally. Josh had had to leave Red Rock in a hurry, pushed on by his cousin, the former Bruce Carter. He had gotten himself mixed up in a penny-ante cattle-rustling deal, and had to leave the country. But, as the drunk described the land, with only one family owning it, he was more than certain it was Luke Kane and his wife, Hannah, who had been married to his cousin, the sheriff.

It was then Josh made the decision to take the valley, with all its rich potential away from Kane, and capitalize upon his holdings.

'Josh Carter is back in the country,' Luke said to Hannah when he returned from his trip into Red Rock. They were at the supper table and she looked up at him, startled.

'Did you see him? Where?'

He shook his head. 'No, but I talked with a fellow that had contacted him recently. He is running with an owl-hoot gang. From what the man said he must have gone bad.'

She was silent for a long moment and then looked at him, her eyes showing her disturbance. 'Do you think he will come here? After all, not many folks know the way into the valley.'

He shrugged. 'I don't know. Somehow that Rawlins found his way here. I suspect

Josh may have somehow figured out how to find us. Maybe it was Josh who told him. Whatever, we'll just have to be ready for anything happening, and deal with it when it comes.'

This is his way, she thought. Concerned, perhaps, but unafraid. All I can do is hope and pray nothing happens to disturb our way of life here. It has been peaceful and fulfilling. However, now and then black clouds do form in the sky. But, for all her thoughts of assurance, a small sense of dread formed in her mind and would not go away.

Kane did not push the matter of Josh Carter away, but it was not priority in his plans and thinking. There was something else more pressing for him and he called the Crow Indian, One Foot, in from where he was breaking a yearling to ride. The old Indian was of a tribe whose livelihood for several centuries depended upon the swiftness of their ponies to run down the buffalo and other animals. The genius of centuries handling wild horses, and bringing them to the hackamore and blanket still lingered in his genes. He was patient, gentle and firm and when he was finished with the animal it was ready to serve him, without having had its spirit broken in the process.

Luke handed the old Indian a twist of tobacco, which One Foot received with a slight nod of thanks.

'Old Friend,' Luke said, 'we may he facing trouble in our valley. Do you know of any trail, any break in the valley walls that would let outsiders in?'

The old Indian stared into the distance as if in deep thought. Then he shook his head. 'I know no such trail or break. But, remember, The Old Ones, what you call *Anasazi*, may have been here long ago, even before my grandfather's grandfather. My nephews and I will look.' Then he turned his attention to Luke, taking his eyes from the distance.

'You know big roan stallion we see with wild ones?'

Luke nodded, his mind still on what One Foot had said about the old ones probably having been in this valley before them. Centuries past these ancients were the fore-runners of the present Indian tribes and culture. They were long gone, but still living in the legends, myths and a complicated culture the remains of which now and then surfaced in the stories of the present Indian tribes.

'Yeah,' he said, 'what about him?'

'A young, red stallion is fighting him for his harem. He's younger, stronger and will one day run the old stallion off and take over the mares. Why don't we snare the roan and leave the young stallion to bring new seed to the herd? We take mares in foal and keep them and their get. Makes fine horses for sell. We get the old roan out, tame him and keep him here and soon we have better foals in our corrals.'

Luke looked at him and nodded slowly and thoughtfully. 'Good thinking, One Foot,' he said. 'You, Black Hawk and Red Feather, get the traps set again over at the springs. We'll see if we can capture that old devil.'

One Foot grunted and nodded. 'Will do,' he said and moved off in his limping stride. Luke had never learned what had happened to the old Indian's left foot. It was but a stub which he kept wrapped in leather. It did not seem to impede his movements, for the old Indian could move along lithely and quickly.

The corral traps at the springs several miles down the valley from the ranch house were ready in a few days after their decision to trap the old stallion and remove him from the scene. His seed was still strong, but the effects of new blood in the herd were important. The four men turned their full attention to the building of the trap.

Trees were cut and brought to the site. The springs were in a small steep-sided arroyo. The far end, just above the spring, was locked by a stand of heavy logs, buried deeply, and then wired together at the center and top. On the far side of the barrier, were braces that would stand hundreds of pounds of pressure. The wild ones caught in such traps fought fiercely to escape, throwing themselves bodily against the logs in their fright and fury.

At the entrance to the trap were two gates, swung from either side, disguised with tree boughs and grasses. The Indians worked diligently, at completing the wild-horse trap by going over the open spaces and brushing the ground with pine boughs, which destroyed their tracks and at the same time took away the man-odors with the pine scent. When it was completed their plan of capture was arrived at in a long evening on the porch of the main house. Hannah and their son, John Lucus, were involved in the planning. They were to handle the gates that would enclose the captured animals. It would be next to impossible to entrap the old stallion singly, for some of his mares would hover about him and would run with him. Undoubtedly they would also be entrapped. This was to be expected, and besides, the mares would be given a quick breaking, and then sold to the army at Laramie.

John Lucus was excited. This would be the first time he'd helped in the capture of the wild ones. That he and his mother had so important a job to perform kept him asking questions and conjuring up scenes during the hours of impatient waiting before the chase of the stallion would begin.

'It won't be easy,' Luke told them. 'That old stallion is wise. He can see traps and outguess us in his own way. But the object is to chase him until he is worn down, and then guide him toward the trap. He'll get thirsty as well as hungry and tired. We'll work him around to where he can scent the springs. He will shy several times. Then he will send the lead mare to the gates and let her signal him if all is well. The mare will go in and drink and when he sees they are undisturbed, his need for the water will overcome his shyness, and he will enter the trap.'

'That's way it's supposed to be,' grunted One Foot. 'We'll be lucky to get him near the trap for a week. But we'll get him,' he nodded. 'We'll get him.'

The drive started.

The herd of wild horses stayed well within their usual territory, two thirds of the way down the valley, among a maze of coulees and steep cliffs, with a myriad of paths leading the way from any place that might hinder their escape as the rancher and his crew moved in on them. Luke and the Indians were in no hurry. They had done this often, and were wise to the ways of the herd. The plan was to wear them down, chase them until they were exhausted. There would be no rest for the herd, nor for those chasing it, Where there was water, the drivers allowed them no time to drink. Where there might be grazing, they were not allowed to graze. Night and day they were driven, and slowly Luke and the Indians guided them subtly back down the valley, away from the brakes and arroyo, toward the springs.

On the day One Foot informed Hannah that the trap would be sprung about sunset, she and John Lucus hid themselves behind the gates, one on either side of the opening to the springs. John Lucus was beside himself with excitement, but the warnings of his father and the old Indian were enough to keep him quiet. His eyes did not move from the flat before the gates over which the wild herd must approach the springs.

And then, suddenly they were there! The old stallion stopped them on a small slope that led down to the springs. He snorted and reared, his eyes searching for signs of trouble. The young stallion that was challenging him for his leadership attempted to force the lead mare down the slope toward the opening to the springs. But the old stallion cut him off, striking out at him with forefeet and bared teeth. The young stallion snorted, tossed his head angrily but gave way to the old stallion one more time.

The stallion paced before his harem, mane tossing in the breeze, tail flaring and twitching in his action, long and flowing to almost sweep the ground. He flared his nostrils and scented the air, knowing that the springs were down there with clear, sweet water, for he had drunk there many times. He neighed, a shrill, challenging bugle. The mares milled behind him.

Finally he made up his mind, driven as he

was by hunger and a deep thirst, for in the days of the chase they had found only small pockets of water here and there among the hills. The entire herd was deeply thirsty, and the mares were nickering softly to him, their nostrils flared, taking in the moist scent of the water that was but a few hundred yards away.

No man could ever detect the signal, but one was given to the lead mare, a deep bay with white markings. Luke had seen her and had thought to capture her for Hannah. Now, moving slowly making certain they did not frighten the animals once they were this close to the trap, he could not see the mare look at the stallion, toss her head and then make her way down the slope and across the small flats to the entrance of the trap.

She paused at the edge of the gate, turning around, from one side to the other, sensing something wrong, but unable to detect its source. The scent of the water was strong now, within her reach, only a few steps away. The moist odor overcame her anxiety; her thirst overriding any other warnings that she might sense, she moved through the gate and slowly approached the edge of the springs. The pool was wide here, sparkling and cool, and she stood before it, still looking about her. Then she stepped forward until she was hock-deep in the water. She tossed her head once, snorted softly, then lowered her lips and drank.

The stallion watched her closely, moving slowly down the slope toward the trap. He saw her enter and that she did not reappear. Prancing before his harem, he tossed his gallant head and signaled them that they could follow their lead mare. He moved back of them, watching, turning, always on the alert, until the last of them had moved through the gates.

Hannah and John Lucus were tensely watching the animals. They were absolutely quiet, the only sounds were of a small breeze teasing the leaves of the aspen above them, the bird-calls that came to them through the bushes and trees. They heard the stamp of the mares' hooves as they moved about the trap, crowding for a place where they could drink.

John Lucus caught his breath.

'There he is!' he whispered to his mother. She nodded and put a finger to her lip. He nodded, his eyes wide and shining as he watched the large animal approach the gate and then, still cautious, suspiciously step inside the trap and then come prancing back. Finally, seeing the mares drinking and peaceful, he moved on into the trap. The lead mare moved aside and back where she could watch for danger. He nosed her flank and then moved in, and lowered his head to the water.

'Now!' Hannah whispered to John Lucus. Quietly, they slipped down from their place of hiding and, each taking hold of the gate, moved it around and across the opening. As they completed closing the trap, Luke came up. With the Indians helping he fastened the gate securely and braced it with poles cut for that purpose; they could only hope that the trap was strong enough to withstand the rushes and fury of the roan stallion when he realized he was trapped and would throw all his weight and energy against the fence and the gate.

'Good job, son,' Luke patted the boy on the back. 'Now we'll see if the trap will hold them.' He turned to One Foot. 'Separate him from the mares as soon as possible. We'll take them to another corral and work with him here alone.'

'That one will be a big job,' One Foot grunted. 'He fight us all the time.'

Luke nodded. 'I know. But with him out of the way, the herd will grow stronger with the new blood of the young stallion. You'll break the roan, I know.'

Hannah had been looking at the mares from a small knoll overlooking the trap. 'There's a beautiful mare, about four years old. I'd like her. She'll make a good riding mare.'

Luke grinned at her. 'I already had her picked out for you,' he said.

Unknown and unsuspected, there was a man with field glasses watching the capture of the wild horses. He turned the glasses and saw the younger stallion herding the remainder of the mares away from danger. Looking again at the captured animals and those moving around the trap, he steadied the glasses suddenly and then gently empowered the focus. There was a woman and her stance and movements were familiar. Hannah! He had found Luke Kane and Hannah. The thought of them, and the hatred of the man he knew to be an ex-Texan Ranger, stirred in him. The years had not lessened his feeling toward Kane, nor had it dimmed but slightly his desire – no, he thought, his lust – for Hannah, formerly the wife of his ex-sheriff cousin, Bruce Carter. For years he had dreamed of having

41

her for himself, but he had never had the nerve to even make his desire known, for Bruce Carter had been a hard, violent, possessive man.

He watched them working with the horses for a long time. Finally he placed the glasses back into a leather pouch, and rose, stretching cramped muscles. He glanced once more down the valley where the horses milled about their trap, turned away and went to his horse, hidden from sight behind a copse of aspen.

Josh Carter was in Paradise Valley, and as he rode away from his hiding place, his mind was casting about as to how he might make the valley – and Hannah – his own.

THREE

Rube Lincoln owned the Lazy L ranch, which lay between the Blue Mesa and the town of Red Rock. Along with his legally proven ownership of thirty thousand acres grazing land, he had access to free government grazing for miles around. His herds numbered in the thousands and his *remuda* was large due to the need for handling, watching and controlling so vast a ranch. Consequently, from time to time it was necessary for him to hire on extra hands to care for the widely spread operation and the huge number of cattle.

When the stranger rode into the ranch and asked for the boss one of the hands working around the tack shed brought him to the main house and turned him over to Rube. The rancher invited the man to be seated on the porch with him, and sent the Mexican woman, wife of a hand and his housekeeper, for coffee.

'I'm Jim Taylor,' the man offered. 'I heard in Red Rock that you might be needing hands for the round-up.

Rube eyed him carefully. About six feet tall, ruddy complexion with sandy hair, rather pale blue eyes. He wore a six-gun on his right thigh, and the rancher noted the butt was well worn, the holster soft and pliant. A shooter? he wondered. There was no need for a gun-hand on the Lazy L. As he scrutinized the man carefully, Rube could not recall ever having seen or heard of him.

'Taylor, eh? You ever worked around here afore?'

Taylor shook his head. 'Nope. Never been

in this part of Wyoming. Been to Laramie a few times, but not this far north and west. You're pretty well back against the Badlands here, as I see it.'

'I've found it a pretty good place to be,' was Rube's answer. He stirred and, standing, looked out over the barns and sheds. 'We're comin' soon on round-up. Guess we can use a good man. If you like it after that, I might find a place for you in my crew for some time. It would be up to you. The foreman's Jesse Garner. He's a good man, but he expects a day's work out of every one who signs on my payroll to do the same.' He turned and eyed Taylor steadily. 'Pay's thirty a month an' found. Got plenty of hosses, so you won't have to use your own except when you want to.'

Taylor was rolling a cigarette. He rose and scratched a match on the porch railing and lighted his smoke, inhaling deeply.

'Sounds about right for me,' he said. 'Do I start right now? If so, point me to the bunkhouse where I can store my possibles, and show me what you want done.'

Rube smiled a slow smile. 'That's the way I like to hear a man talk. Come on, I'll show you around an' if Jess is around I'll turn you over to him.'

The work with the wild horses went well.

'We'll have a good bunch of mares to take into Red Rock in a week or two,' Luke told Hannah over breakfast a few weeks after the capture of the horses. 'That old roan stallion, however, is making us work. He doesn't like anything he sees, hears, or smells. It's gonna be a long job getting him just to where he'll not try to beat down the poles of a corral.'

'Are we all going to Red Rock?' asked John Lucus, his eyes shining, his thoughts far ahead already planning on what he could do with the time in the town. Hannah glanced at Luke and smiled.

'I seem to recall that there is to be a round-up dance and that it is during the time we plan to be in town. Perhaps we *can* all go.'

'That's right,' Luke nodded. 'And it was what I was hoping might be possible. There was an item in the paper I brought back with me telling about the dance. There's about fifteen mares and colts ready for sale. I'll telegraph Laramie army post and they'll send someone up to buy the animals.'

Going into Red Rock was an occasion not only for the boy, but for the grown ups as well. It gave opportunity to meet again and talk with friends and acquaintances to enjoy the give and take of news of the area and of the territory; of how the issue was going in the capital as to when Wyoming would become a state, of rustlers that kept nibbling away at herds, of the price of beef, and all those everyday items that guided their existence.

Leading three packhorses, Luke and Hannah with John Lucus darting here and there on his piebald pony, left the valley in the hands of One Foot and his nephews. They made their way through the narrow entrance to the valley and once there, they camped in a line-shack while the Indians sent the mares and colts through the narrow gap in the mesa wall. As the animals came out of the gap on to the mesa, Hannah and Luke milled them and held them in a small cul-de-sac until the Indians came through and helped them keep the horses bunched.

While Hannah and the Indians waited, Kane continued to the Lazy L ranch of Rube Lincoln, a close friend, and brought back with him three hands to help haze the horses across the range to Red Rock. There they were corraled and Kane sent his telegram to Fort Robinson outside Laramie, asking for a representative to come look over the herd.

Jim Taylor was one of the three Lazy L hands sent to help with the herd of half-wild, half-tamed horses. Introduced to Kane, he surveyed the ex-Ranger closely, noting that Luke was not armed, but that his cool, direct way of working with the men spoke of his abilities and his strengths. Observing these qualities, Taylor did not doubt the stories of his ability with a six-gun. Taylor recalled the words of Josh Carter. Don't let his quietness and coolness fool you. He can explode in a moment and when he does things about him become involved.

Taylor was in Red Rock for one purpose. He had gotten the job with the Lazy L ranch so that he might be in proximity of Kane at some given point of time, and Carter had explained to him: 'Watch him, choose your time, and get him! Keep him occupied in Red Rock for the entire time of the round-up dance and party, and in the meantime me and the boys will take over the valley. Far as I can see he had just three Injuns working for him, and they won't be nothing to take care of.'

'I hear there's only one way into the valley,

47

through a gap so narrow that one man could hold off an army. How are we gonna get in there without trouble?'

Josh had grinned and tapped his forehead with a finger. 'I know another way. Trust me. We'll get into the valley. When you get back from Red Rock, the valley will be ours and Luke Kane will be dead.'

The town was ready for the round-up dance. There was a dance platform erected between the schoolhouse and the livery stable. Lanterns were erected on poles at all four corners of the platform, and others erected on all four sides of the structure. A railing ran around the flat surface, with a small opening at one end. Those going on to the floor left their guns at a table just outside the opening, and tossed a free-will offering into a box, the money to be used for school books and other items for the school. The dance was to begin at sundown the day following the end of the round-up, which was this particular day that Luke Kane brought his herd into town to sell, and his family to enjoy the occasion.

Hannah and Kane instructed Lucus what to do and not to do, as parents have done eternally, and then went their own ways,

48

knowing the boy would stay within the bounds of the city and that he would not get into any more trouble than any other eight-year-old boy. He gave a final pat to Lucus's shoulder and watched with a smile as the lad scurried off towards the dance platform where undoubtedly he would meet peers with the same goals in mind.

Hannah kissed him on the cheek and admonished. 'Try to keep out of trouble, Luke. It seems to follow you around.'

He grinned. 'You may be right, but you wouldn't want me to turn tail and run every time some ranny braces me, would you?' She made a face at him and left to go to George Holt's mercantile. There she was greeted by the owner of the store.

'Hannah Kane! I was wondering if you and your family would be in for the dance.'

She smiled at him and for a short time, between customers, they had small talk about the community and friends. Then she looked at him with a question.

'George, is your apartment upstairs still open?'

He nodded. 'Yep. In fact I anticipated you might be in for the fracas and I had it cleaned and aired out, hopin' you would want it.'

Hannah had lived in the apartment years past, when she and her first husband, the former sheriff of Red Rock, had parted ways. From time to time during the past years she and Luke had come into town, and stayed in the apartment.

'I'll take some things up, if you don't mind,' she told him. 'We'll be there at least three nights.'

He handed her a key. 'It's yours, Hannah, anytime you want it. Just come in an' ask.'

Jim Taylor, following Luke and Hannah at a distance, stood on the porch of the Red Rock saloon and watched her climb the stairs to the apartment.

'A lush piece,' he mused. 'Wonder if Kane is keeping her happy. Maybe, just maybe...' He built a picture of himself and Hannah together, then shook it off, and turning, entered the saloon. Seated at a table was a man waiting for him. Jim Taylor had brought him in from Josh Carter's gang. He was not about to face former Ranger, Luke Kane, by himself. Rob Ballard looked up as Taylor entered through the bat-winged door.

Taylor bought himself a beer and seated himself across the table from Ballard.

'This dance comin' up tonight is just the

right time for us to brace Kane. Josh said to rough him up good, and if push comes to shove, kill him. But get it done this evening, for Josh and the boys are goin' to make their move in the morning.'

Ballard was a small man. Dark of feature, with a sharp nose and thin lips that seemed never to have known a smile. His eyes were large in a small face, dark and unfathomable. His face remained stoic regardless of the conversation.

'Where can I find this ranny so's I can size him up? I don't like to go into a fracas cold turkey. I like to have a little edge, if possible.'

Taylor nodded. 'He's down at the tack show right now. I suspect he'll be in for a drink in a little while. Then you will have a good chance to look him over at the corrals back of the livery for he brought in some hosses to sell. The army will probably take them all for mounts. So he'll probably be down there most of the day afore the dance begins. Then him an' his wife will be there to swing a set or two.'

Ballard nodded. 'What are you goin' to be doin' whilst I'm takin' care of this so-called wildcat?'

'Oh, don't worry,' Taylor stretched in the chair and pushed back his hat. 'I'll be

51

backin' you up a hundred per cent.' He grinned at Ballard. 'But you get to do the real work, an' that will put you in real good with the boss.'

Ballard snorted. 'I don't need Josh Carter. He ain't got much backbone. But I want a slice of the pie when he sells the beef he's after, an' whatever tamed hosses he gets when he takes over that valley ranch. Beyond that ... who knows?'

The two men had another beer, Taylor buying, and then parted. Ballard left the saloon and made his way to the corrals back of the livery. It was mid-afternoon, and the place was hot and dusty with the milling horses. Leaning against the top corral rail, Ballard watched the animals and thought over what he was supposed to do for Josh Carter. Bruise Luke Kane up real good? Why bother? He, himself, was no match physically for Kane. Kane was taller, heavier, and an experienced fighter with his fists, so he was told. *He* stood about five feet six inches in his boots. So the idea of meeting Kane in a physical free-for-all fistfight was stupid. And hire some roustabout to waylay and backshoot him from some alley? Ballard shook his head. Somehow he would force him into a gunfight and kill him, legally, before a crowd. As he mused and watched, Kane came from the livery to the corrals, walking with a uniformed soldier. It was an officer, Ballard saw, detecting the glint of silver on his shoulders.

Kane glanced over at him and Ballard had the feeling that those green eyes saw everything they wanted to see in that one sweeping glance. He waited until Kane's interest was again centered on the horses, talking with the officer who was questioning him, and pointing at this mare and that colt. He slipped away and returned to the saloon. He bought his drink and found a table near the back wall across the room from the door. As he walked away, the bartender noted something rather unusual about the man.

His weapon, on his right hip, was carried low, and it was tied with leather thongs about his thigh. He sighed and shook his head. Trouble coming.

This man was a shootist.

FOUR

Josh Carter was in Paradise Valley.

He knew about the narrow and almost secret entrance to the valley owned and occupied by Luke Kane. He was also aware that a man with a good rifle could hold off a small army indefinitely if the entrance was attacked. But now he no longer spent long hours planning how to enter the valley that way. He had found another entrance.

A wandering rider of the owl-hoot trails had described to him an old trail over a lower pass in the lower end of the valley, miles from Luke's stronghold near the narrowed pass through the mesa wall.

'It's dim, it's rough, hardly a trail a-tall,' the man said. And for a quart of hard liquor he had drawn Josh a map, detailed and crude, but enough for Josh to follow and bring in a crew of ten men beside himself and Jim Taylor, who was in Red Rock keeping tabs on Luke Kane. Taylor had orders also to cripple Kane badly, enough to take him out of the scene while Josh and his crew could raid the valley ... or *eliminate* him!

He brought his riders down out of the mountains and into the valley proper and led them to within a mile of the headquarters of the ranch. There, while the rest waited in the shade of a copse of slim pines and aspen, he rode to just below the crown of a slope. He dismounted and walked to the peak, keeping low and under cover of brush.

He eyed the ranch buildings and corrals with a pair of army field-glasses, gotten following the War, and saw that there were no hands about. The roan stallion paced restlessly about the single corral enclosing him. There were perhaps a dozen mares and fillies in the larger holding corrals, but beyond that he detected no movement about the ranch. Kane and his family had gone into Red Rock for the dance.

He slid back down to his mount, and leading the horse returned to the crew.

'It's clear,' he said. He mounted and turned the horse towards the ranch house. 'Let's go. We'll be in and out and it will be another twelve hours, maybe longer, before Kane is back and knows he has had visitors.'

'An' then what?' asked one of the riders,

pulling his horse up beside his boss.

'Then we'll see how much sand the great Luke Kane has in his pants. I want that man, if he comes back from Red Rock. He might not, you know.' He smirked at the rider. He slapped his reins against the neck of the horse. 'Come on, let's get it done.'

Black Hawk, the younger of One Foot's nephews came loping down from the shelf before the entrance to the valley. One Foot was in the tack shed, preparing to work with the roan when the young Indian came running to him.

'Riders come,' he said. One Foot whirled about and looked up at the wall where the entrance led on to the shelf into the valley. 'No not there,' Black Hawk said. He gestured with his chin toward the lower corrals and the few half-broken animals. 'Dust over there.'

A fine swirl of dust, hardly discernible to the eye, seeming like a fog, drifted upward from a point a few miles beyond the lower corrals and the creek.

One Foot studied it momentarily and then quickly gave orders. 'You hide, let them do what they goin' to do. Then you follow.'

Black Hawk nodded.

'Red Feather will stay at the wall entrance,' One Foot added. 'I will go into Red Rock and find Kane and tell him.'

With that the Indians parted and disappeared from the corral. Josh Carter did not detect their presence. Ages of stalking wild game for food, centuries of training how to observe an enemy without being observed, flowed in the blood of the Indians. Black Hawk's keen eyes followed every movement of the outlaw crew as they came into sight. He noted and remembered faces, dress, horses they rode, and what they did. Luke Kane would get a detailed report when he returned.

Within a few minutes of the riders arriving at the ranch corrals, the mares and fillies were hazed from their corral and headed toward the far end of the valley. Josh Carter rode to the corral that held the roan stallion. The big animal shied to the far side of the corral and eyed him, ears laid flat back against his head. Josh realized it would take a lot of time and several of his crew to conquer the horse and then lead him to a cul-de-sac. There he intended to hold the horses and beef until he could take them across the pass he had discovered and on to a shipping-point where no questions would be asked.

He rode up before the beautiful log-and-stucco house Kane and Hannah had struggled to build. He noted the cleanliness of the surround area, the flower beds, a large vegetable garden back of the house. For an instant he was tempted to toss a lighted bunch of sage grass into the house and watch it burn to the ground. But time was passing. He grimaced and then shrugged. For now the beef and the horses was enough. More would come later. And if Jim Taylor did what he was supposed to do or have done in Red Rock, then the valley was already Carter's!

Signaling to the rider with him, he left the yard of the house, deliberately trampling a flower bed as he left. It was just another signature that he had been there!

He followed his crew, catching up with the drags, and then loped on to the head of the drive. He would lead them to the holding place himself and there wait for Taylor's report.

The dance at Red Rock had begun at dark.

The lanterns were lighted about the dance floor. Musicians were tuning guitars and fiddles and mandolins. There was no bass fiddle, but one man had purchased a new two-gallon jug and was puffing and blowing on it, to achieve the deep sounds needed for background to the other instruments.

The crowd was gathering; in fact, had been gathering since noon. It was one of the few times in the territory for the citizens to gather and visit and enjoy a relaxation away from the everyday drudgery of life on the frontier. The only other occasion for a party, other than a dance-party, was a hanging and there had been no neck-tie parties for several months. Clarence Holland, the sheriff of Red Rock and surrounding territory, was present from the beginning. There would be some cowboys off the ranges now that round-up was over, who would take this occasion to enjoy some rowdy activities, drinking to staggering drunkenness, some belligerent and ready to fight just for the fun of it. Holland was determined that they would have a good time, but that rough stuff, fist-fighting and other tests of prowess and manhood, would not be tolerated. He and two appointed deputies would soon have the trouble-makers in jail for an overnight stay. He also, while armed himself, was adamant that all weapons would be checked at a table before the individual could enter the entertainment area. There would be, and were, grumbles at this shucking off of their individual weapons, but he would brook no argument. His word was final at this point. Check your guns, knives and brass knuckles, or stay away.

Rob Ballard stood with Jim Taylor in the shadows of the livery watching the crowd gather.

'This is about the only time you'll get a good chance at Kane,' Taylor told the gunman. 'I'll back you up. An' I'll watch the sheriff and the deputies. You concentrate on Kane.'

'I've been told he's pretty good with a six-gun,' Ballard said.

'Yeah, so have I,' said Taylor, 'but from what I know about you, you're faster than he is, an' besides, you'll have the edge of bracing him, without him expectin' anything.'

During the afternoon, as he worked at the corrals with the army representative, Luke noticed Rob Ballard leaning on the top poles watching the proceedings. He noted the tied down six-gun on the right hip and

60

the fact that Ballard seemed more interested in studying him and his movements, than he did in the sale of mares and fillies to the army.

Luke Kane had hung up his six-gun years ago. At the present he carried it only when out on the range, where it might be useful against some angered wild animal, or against a vicious range bull who was defiant to the point of charging a man on a horse, hazing him from some hiding place in a brush-filled coulee. The reason for his not arming himself for any other occasions came from his past as a Texas Ranger when he was forced to fire upon a boy, just in his middle teens, when the boy charged him with a knife. Two men and the boy were rustling specially bred beef when Kane discovered them. Rather than surrender to him, and face prison, they elected to fight, and the youngster was killed.

Kane regretted this deeply. So much so that he left the Rangers and went into ranch work. He hung up his six-gun, so to speak, when it came to anything other than range work in the valley where danger might lurk in any copse of trees, hidden brakes or brush covered slopes.

This did not mean that he was no longer

proficient with the six-gun. He, and his son, John Lucus, spent time in target practice with both six-gun and rifle, Kane teaching the boy the art of caring for a good weapon, as well as how to use it, when necessary. They hunted in the mountains surrounding the valley, and John Lucus, at age eight, was a good shot with the rifle and with a smaller caliber of pistol.

Kane left the corrals with the army representative, and went into the livery, where his horse was stabled. He took from his blanket roll on the cantle of the saddle his gun belt and six-gun, a .44 Colt revolver. Thoughtfully he swung it about his waist and settled it in place. He slid the weapon out of the leather a few times to assure its free movement, and left the livery to find Hannah and John Lucus. Also, he was looking for Clarence Holland, the sheriff, to see if he had any further rumors of Josh Carter being in the territory. He met the sheriff on the boardwalk before the saloon.

'How about a beer before the party gets under way?' the sheriff asked Kane.

'Well, seein' as you invited me, I reckon that means you're payin'?' Kane grinned at Holland.

'Maybe for the first one,' the sheriff

grinned. 'After that you're spendin' some of that wild-horse money you're collecting from the US Army.'

'You're on.' Kane held open the bat-wing doors of the saloon and stepped aside for the sheriff to precede him. They lined up at the bar and in a few minutes were sipping their brew, passing on remarks about daily occurrences both in the town and from the ranch.

Holland glanced at Kane's gun belt. 'I see you're packin' again. How come?'

Kane sipped his beer and then answered softly. 'There's a ranny in town that seems always to be about when I'm out, whether in the livery, at the corrals, or' – he nodded to a table in the rear of the room – 'here. I don't know him, but he's wearin' tied down iron, an' looks and acts like a gunnie.'

Holland casually turned his head and looked at Rob Ballard, who was seated at the table Kane had indicated. He turned back to Luke. 'Never saw him afore, but you're right. He's wearin' a six-gun like he wants to be ready to use it any time. Reckon I'll just have a little confab with him.'

When Luke left the saloon to find Hannah and John Lucus, the sheriff set his mug down on the bar and sauntered over to the table where Ballard sat looking broodingly

63

at the doorway where Kane had just exited.

The sheriff paused before the table, his eyes fastened on Ballard's face. The man slowly looked up, eyeing the lawman calmly.

'Howdy, Sheriff. What can I do for you? Join me in a beer?'

Holland shook his head. 'Nope, thanks anyway. I just finished a couple.' He pointed to the chair opposite Ballard. 'Care if I set down?'

Ballard shrugged. 'Most sheriffs of most towns don't ask, they just squat. Sure, pull up a chair. What's on your mind?'

'You're a stranger in town. I'm not only sheriff of the territory around here, but I am the law in Red Rock, as well. There will be no gunplay in my town. Now, I know there will be some rough stuff, boys just out of the round-up, money in their pockets, and willingness to have a rousin' good time. That's all well and good. I'm for it ... within bounds. Now you bein' new here, I thought you just might like to know some ground rules.'

Ballard listened with calm eyes on the sheriff's face. Finally he nodded. 'I'm a peaceful man, Sheriff. You won't have no trouble with me. But I don't back away from trouble if it comes at me. Just so you understand that.'

Holland was not satisfied. There was something about the man, his attitude, his calm acceptance of the sheriff's rules of conduct while he was in Red Rock. They seemed to slip off the man's attention, as a shrug would disregard some wayward remark. The sheriff rose and leaned across the table, eye to eye with Ballard.

'This is my town. You cause no trouble and there'll be no trouble from me. Cause it an' I'll be on you like a maw cow guardin' her calf. An' if you go to the dance, you behave like a gentleman. We treat our women folk about here with respect and courtesy.'

A light flared momentarily in Ballard's eyes, and then quieted. He nodded. 'Like I said, Sheriff, you'll have no trouble from me.'

Luke and Hannah walked down the main street to the platform where the dance was beginning to form. Square-dance sets were being paired off, the musicians tuned and ready. Couples were approaching the entry to the dance floor, each tossing a coin in the box where the weapons were checked. Acquaintances saw them approach and called to them.

'Come on, Luke. Bring that pretty lady with you, an' fill out our square-dance set. We need another couple to fill it.'

Luke waved. 'Be right there, Hank. Hannah here is pinin' to teach me how to shake a leg. So I reckon I'll give in, this time.' Hannah gave him a playful shove.

Luke and Hannah were soon stepping lively in the first square-dance of the evening. John Lucus, finding boys of his own age, was soon scurrying around, climbing nearby trees, slipping beneath the tables and snitching cookies, doing all those things a boy will do while parents are otherwise occupied.

The first set finished, the musicians moved into a slow waltz, 'Over the Waves', and couples danced closely to the sweeter music. Hannah moved in Luke's arms, her eyes shining up into his. Her lips moved close to his ear and whispered, and he nodded and smiled, blushing at her remark that he was the best dancer on the floor, and that all the girls were just waiting for a break, hoping he would leave Hannah for one waltz, and ask one of them.

Clarence Holland stood in the shadows of the livery stable and watched. He saw Rob Ballard standing on the far side of the dance floor, talking with Jim Taylor, who the sheriff knew was working for the Lazy L. Why were they talking? Casual meeting? Know each other from the past? He watched them and saw that their eyes turned frequently to where Luke Kane danced with his wife, or for a brief time with one of the other women, while Hannah was claimed by another man for a dance. Luke had mentioned that everywhere he had gone in Red Rock, Ballard seemed to always be close by. What was on his mind? The sheriff watched them, a slight dread or thought of approaching trouble moving into his consciousness.

The dance ceased at last, the musicians asking for a break, and a chance to visit a place where a jug was being passed about. An individual from off the range was doing a brisk business off the tail end of his buckboard; home-made beer, some raw, recently pressed wine, as well as a mug of 'pop skull', corn liquor made with his own hands.

'I'm going to take a minute,' he told Hannah, 'to locate John Lucus and check on the horses. I'll be right back.' She squeezed his hand and turned to her conversation with a ranch wife she had known for years, and had seen only occasionally at such occasions as this.

Luke moved to the table where the weapons were checked and, finding his own belt with the six-gun, buckled it about his waist. He left the dance area and moved up the street, his eyes searching the shadows, the alleys opening on to Main Street, the porches of buildings. John Lucus came from between two buildings and waved to him.

'Playin' hide-an'-seek, Dad,' he called, disappearing quickly into the shadows of another building. Kane nodded approval to his son and continued toward the corrals.

Rob Ballard left Jim Taylor, where they were standing on the far side of the dance platform. He followed Kane up the street, until suddenly he did not see the tall figure of the ex-Ranger before him. He hesitated and then picked up his stride, attempting to keep Kane in his sight. He turned the corner of the livery, moving slowly now, looking this way and that, his hand on the butt of his six-gun. There was the sound of a step behind him, and he whirled to look into the face of Luke Kane.

'Was you lookin' for me, Ballard? Well, here I am. Speak your piece an' get it out of your craw.'

Ballard stiffened. He spread his legs, his right hand against his gunbelt above the butt of his six-gun.

'You are mine, Kane! Go for your gun!'

FIVE

Josh Carter gloried in the fact that he and his crew had managed to get away from the Kane ranch without being seen, and on the way back to the lower reaches of the valley with the mares and fillies he had taken, they gathered up at least three hundred head of cattle. It was a bawling, whinnying, kicking, protesting mixture of beef and horseflesh he drove into a small valley, a cul-de-sac, not far from his campsite, but well out of sight of anyone riding casually through the area. Wind soon obliterated the tracks of the herd, and well away from the trail through the center of the valley, the sound of the animals could not be heard.

He crowded the mares into a small coulee, where there was a small stream, and where some lush grasses covered the small area. This would keep them fed and watered until they could be driven out of the valley and taken to an unscrupulous dealer who would not question brands or former ownership. As he worked with the crew, he wondered how Jim Taylor and Ballard were doing in Red Rock, in the confrontation with Luke Kane.

However, in his feelings about obscurity, and success in getting away with the herd unseen, he was wrong. Black Hawk followed them to the cul-de-sac. He was trained in tracking, his keen eyesight kept him abreast of their movement, and his Indian instinct at concealment allowed him to remain much closer to the rustlers than any white man might have been able to do.

Carter eyed the beef they had rustled. He noted the Lazy L brand on the hips of the animals, but shrugged. The person he was selling them to, certainly for less than top dollar, since he knew they were rustled, would shrug at the brand. He and his crew would alter the brands and sell quickly. Beef for the growing population of the Eastern cities, was beef to the man; brands were shrugged off. Money talked.

Carter and one of his crew moved on to the small coulee, where the few mares and fillies were being held. He, watching them, mused: they were not fully broken. He saw none he liked, other than a bay mare which looked to be four years old.

'Rope her out,' he told the ranny with him. 'Then turn the rest of them loose. It won't be long before that red stallion we saw a few days ago will have them rounded up and in his harem. We ain't got time to fool with 'em.'

'Yeah,' the cowboy agreed. 'An' there ain't no one in our bunch can break wild ones like these.'

Carter nodded. 'Rope out that mare I pointed out to you. We'll see what we can do with her. If she's impossible, we'll turn her loose, too.'

Carter was more than pleased with the day's work. He had raided the stronghold of his enemy, stolen his horses, taken a small herd of what he could see were prime cattle, and in doing so left a challenge to Kane. Kane had no large crew. It would be weeks before he figured out what had become of the animals. Then while he was away, searching for them, Carter would burn his headquarters, and maybe, just maybe, bring Hannah along with him. He visioned what he might do to and with her and licked his lips in anticipation.

He rode back to the campsite, dismounted, and turned the horse over to a handler to corral and rub down. He went into the campsite, where three of his crew were erecting a windbreak with pine poles, tarps and building a furnace in front of the structure for cooking and for reflected warmth on cold nights. High up as he was, the days were warm, but the night chilled down. He poured himself a cup of coffee from the ever-present pot of the strong brew, and sipping it, looked about. He motioned his *segundo*, Milo Swartz, to join him.

'Today was the day of the shindig at Red Rock, wasn't it?'

Swartz stepped over, and refilling his coffee tin, nodded. 'Yup. Rob Ballard an' Jim Taylor both are supposed to be there. By the way, Buck Leonard come back.' Swartz grinned through his jagged teeth. 'He looks like a herd of buffalo run over him.'

Carter grimaced. 'Maybe Taylor and Ballard will be able to bring Luke Kane to the ground.'

But he had another report not in yet.

John Lucus Kane might be eight years old, but he was an observing youngster. He looked back from his hiding place in the alley and heard Rob Ballard challenge his father. He saw them both taking a stance that spelled only one thing to him. His father was being pushed into a gunfight!

Fear striking through him for his father, he raced down the alley, around back of the saloon, and across the street to where the dance platform was being filled again for the next dance. He saw his mother talking with the sheriff and getting ready to join another man for the next set. He yelled.

'Mom ... Mom! Dad's in trouble! Come on right now!'

Sheriff Holland saw John Lucus, and stepped out to confront the boy who was racing toward his mother. 'Here, boy. What's this about trouble?'

Hannah hurried down the steps from the platform and joined them. 'What is it, John Lucus?' she asked, anxiously. 'What about your father?'

Trembling; the boy pointed back up the street. 'There's a man, wearin' a gun, that stopped Dad on the way to the livery, I guess. An' it looks like he's makin' Dad fight him.'

The sheriff took off in a run, and several men, hearing what the boy had said, followed him. Hannah hugged her son and soothed him. 'Come on, now, we'll go to see what it's all about,' she told him. Her heart was pounding with fear, however, for she had experienced these moments previously, when her man was challenged. Luke Kane did not seek trouble, but his former experiences, as a Texas Ranger, had drawn those seeking a name for themselves as gunmen, and for the misplaced pride of having bested one whose name was mentioned among those of the Earp brothers, Ben Thompson, Hickok and others.

They sought him out to make a name for themselves, and up to the present had found themselves being measured for a six-foot box, or at least wounded severely enough for their desire to become a shootist, become history. This she knew as she ran with the sheriff and her son to where her husband was facing a gunman.

Rob Ballard was somewhat nonplussed. There was no fear on the countenance of the man facing him. In fact, he seemed to have a relaxed attitude. Only his eyes reflected alertness. His right hand hung beside the butt of his six-gun, he seemed to be brooding about what was to happen.

'I never draw first. I don't even know who

you are, your name. Why should I fight you? For if I do one of us will not walk away from here.'

The calmness and surety of his voice, low-pitched but carrying, caused a tenseness to grip Ballard, as never before when he squared away for a gunfight. There seemed to be more to this man than Josh Carter or Jim Taylor had indicated. Momentarily a cautionary doubt fleeted through his mind, and then his pride and the knowledge of his own expertise at this business reassured him.

'If that's the way you want it,' he gritted, his eyes narrowing and his right hand tensing over his gun butt. Suddenly something began to happen which he had never experienced before. Kane began a slow walk toward him, his face still calm, expressionless. Ballard was shaken.

'That's far enough. I'll kill you right this moment. Stand still and draw!'

As he spoke his right hand slashed down to his gun butt and lifted the weapon from the leather. He was fast and he jerked off a round. The gun blasted and the bullet dug into the ground at Kane's feet. He yelled at Kane, and immediately triggered another round.

As Ballard's weapon roared Kane's hand moved, a blur of movement. Kane turned sideways to his opponent and leveled his weapon quickly but steady. Ballard leveled his pistol for the second round, and as he pulled the trigger, Kane fired. The bullet from Ballard's weapon whistled by his hat brim, missing by mere inches.

Kane fired one shot. His pistol level, his eyes watching intently and the hammer eared back for another blast, he paused. Ballard stood straight, his face paling with shock. Kane's round had bored through his lungs and torn its way through the chest cavity, emerging with a burst of blood from the man's back. Ballard's hand dropped and the six-gun fell into the dust of the street, slipping from his lax fingers. He staggered back, losing balance, and then as death took him in its dark shroud, he fell to the street. His body stiffened momentarily and quivered, and then relaxed, as life left it for all time.

Slowly Kane walked over and looked down at his erstwhile opponent. His toe nudged the six-gun further away from the body. His eyes brooded as he slowly poked the empty cartridge to the ground, and his fingers automatically pulled a round from his gunbelt and slipped it in to the empty chamber.

'Dad!' John Lucus came racing up the street and threw his arms around his father's legs. 'Dad! I was so scared!' Luke placed his hand on his son's head and turned him toward the boardwalk.

'Oh, Luke ... Luke!' Hannah was in his arms pressing her head against his chest. 'I was so afraid.' She hid her face on his vest, not looking at the body in the street. He held her close and breathed deeply for the first time since the fight had begun.

The sheriff was right behind Hannah and stood looking down at the body. 'Did you know him?' he asked Luke.

Kane shook his head. 'Never saw him before in my life,' he said. 'Maybe you can find some identification on him. He never said anything, just called me out.'

George Holt, the mercantile owner, stepped up. 'I was in my store puttin' up some supplies,' he told the sheriff. 'I heard that man there,' he pointed to Ballard's body, 'challenge Luke. An' he drawed first. He was earin' back for his last shot when Luke drawed. It was purely self-defense. I saw and heard it all.'

The sheriff nodded. He looked at Kane.

'Luke, I've knowed you for over ten years now, or more, an' it seems like trouble just waits for you to arrive.' He shook his head. 'Why people get it into their heads that it's important to be better than someone else I'll never understand. I think this is just a ranny who was purty slick with a pistol an' heard you, Luke, was a former Ranger, and good with a pistol. He decided to notch his six-gun an' then brag how he bested you. That's probably the reason he called you out.' He motioned to his deputy. 'Get some men an' tote this body down to Doc Somers. Whatever he had on him will pay fer a place on Boot Hill.'

Hannah took Luke's hand. 'Come on, honey. Let's go to the rooms and get some rest. I'll make you a cup of coffee and you can take a bath.' She pulled him close to her. 'Why anyone would want to shoot a fine man like yourself, I'll never know, and if I can help it, no one will ever get another chance at you. I'm going to keep you pinned up on that valley of ours from now on.'

Luke put his arm about her as they moved towards the stairs that reached up to the apartment over the mercantile. John Lucus joined them, subdued at this moment, over what had just occurred. His dad ruffled his hair. 'You done just fine, Lucus. Just fine. We're proud of you.'

Jim Taylor stayed in the background. He was disconcerted that Ballard had failed in his attempt to take out Luke Kane. Josh Carter would fume again. It seemed that every time he had what he deemed a good chance of besting Kane, it turned out bad. Taylor drew a deep breath. Best he get out of Red Rock and back to the Lazy L, before someone remembered seeing him and Ballard talking.

It was midnight when there came a soft knocking at the apartment door. Hannah heard it first and nudged Luke. He moved quickly and quietly from the bed, his pistol in hand and went to the door.

'Who is it?' he called, his ear against the door.

'One Foot,' came the guttural reply. 'Bad things happen at ranch. You come.'

SIX

Jim Taylor stood beside the hut in Carter's campsite, rolling a cigarette and listening to Carter's tirade.

'I send Buck Leonard to find Luke Kane and rough him up and give him a message, and instead Buck is used to wipe up the streets of Red Rock. Then I send you and Rob Ballard in to bring him down and you come back to tell me that he killed Ballard. What's goin' on here? Do I have a bunch of panty-waists riding' with me? Why can't one of you bring down one man?'

Taylor lit his cigarette and blew smoke towards his boss. 'Why don't you go in and brace him yourself? If you think you're better than any of us, then why are you sendin' someone else to do the job for you?'

'That why you get a cut in whatever we do together?' Josh snarled. 'You got your cut in the bank job, didn't you? You got your cut out of the beef we rustled and sold this past year, didn't you? That's why I sent you in, to do a job for the crew as well as yourselves.'

Taylor straightened, his eyes cold. He drew the last of the smoke from the cigarette and flipped it insolently at Carter's feet. 'I will brace a man when I want to. But it looks like the only way you can take Luke Kane out of the picture, is to back-shoot him, an' I won't do that fer any man.'

Carter glared at him and tensed, as though to carry the situation a step further. Then he relaxed and shrugged. 'No need for us to get riled up, Jim,' he said, his voice subsiding into casual tones. 'Go get your supper. We'll have a confab about our next step this evenin'. Glad you're back.'

He turned and walked away, still fuming inside, but knowing that he had neither the expertise with a pistol to challenge Taylor, nor did he actually have the nerve to do so. Josh Carter was a coward at heart, and he was aware of it. That he kept sending others to confront an old enemy, Luke Kane, attested to that fact.

The next morning, after having decided to move the cattle and horses to a railhead for shipment before Kane could return, he walked away from the camp to a higher point where he could over-look the valley. It was indeed a paradise. There was graze, there was water, there was timber. Kane had stumbled upon this and acquired it for himself. Josh had traveled to the territorial capital and inquired as to the possibility of acquiring the valley – for himself legally, to find that Kane had filed claim on the valley years before, and grazing rights of government- and state-owned property about the valley, was his to use if and when necessary. Josh was furious. That Kane seemed to best him at every turn was deeply galling. Now ... just maybe, he might get an upper hand on Kane. He nodded to himself; it just might happen.

On his way back down a series of coulees to his camp, he noticed a dark opening to one side of the animal track he was following. He paused, pushed aside some small bushes and saw the opening of what must be a small cave. Such places often housed rattlesnakes, bears of that part of the country, and now and then a cougar. Seizing a handful of sagebrush he lighted it, and tossed it as far into the cave as possible from where he stood. He stepped back and waited, his six-gun in his hand. No telling what might come bursting out of the cave. But after several minutes he decided the cavern was unoccupied.

Stooping, he entered the cave, holding a

torch of twisted sagebrush in one hand and his six-gun in the other. Once he was a few steps beyond the entrance, the cave opened up into a large cavern, the ceiling beyond the flickering light of his torch, the sides widely apart. Seeing a piece of wood on the floor before him, he lighted it from the now dying torch, and slowly moved about the cave.

It was dry. One wall, a sheer drop of sandstone, showed dimly sketched figures of animals and humans. He paid little attention to them, but looked questioningly at a circle of stones, in which were blacked remains of fire. He bent to touch one remaining piece of material and it crumbled to dust in his fingers. Ancient remains of a camp-fire, circled by fire and smoke-blackened stones told him the cave had not been occupied for years. Looking about him once again, an errant thought came to him; he pushed it away and, the torch dying, made his way to the entrance and left the cavern.

Once outside he paused; he pushed the bushes back against the entrance, pulled some bunch-grass and scattered it about, leaving the cave opening concealed to any but a discerning eye. Pleased with what he had found and with his manner of concealing it, he proceeded down to the campsite. Several of the crew were about, but none seemed to have taken notice of his absence.

That evening, as they completed their meal, he stood and spoke to them.

'The time's come. We take the herd out tomorrow. Jim, you handle the beef. I'll be with the *remuda*. Take them over the trail slow, for it's rough and dangerous. But when you get through push them hard to the railhead. We may lose some weight, but I want to get them there and out of the country.'

One Foot stood at the door of the apartment looking at Kane.

'Bad things happen at ranch. You come now.'

'What kind of bad things?' Kane asked, reaching for his shirt. He had jerked on his pants before he opened the door. Hannah sat up in bed, covers up to her shoulders, staring at the Indian. On a cot across the room John Lucus stirred at the commotion then turned and dropped off to sleep again.

'What is it, Luke?' asked Hannah, peering past Luke to the open door. There was no light in the room other than that coming in from a starlit night.

'Tell me about the ranch,' Luke said. 'What's happening that would bring you out here in the middle of the night?'

'Men come and take horses. They tried to take roan stallion, but was too much trouble, I betcha. Roan put up a fight. Black Hawk followed them. Red Feather guard pass into the valley.'

Luke turned to Hannah. 'Get dressed,' he said, 'and get John Lucus up and ready to go.' He turned to One Foot. 'We'll meet you at the Lazy L and decide what to do from there.'

'Me go,' grunted the Indian, and disappeared into the night. Luke looked at his wife.

'We have to go right now. Something has happened at the ranch. Someone is rustling our horses, and I suspect our cattle as well. We'll go to the Lazy L and sort it all out.'

In a few minutes they were dressed and hurrying to the livery. They roused the liveryman out of his nest and were soon mounted. Luke leaned down from the saddle and motioned the liveryman to him.

'Come morning, you go tell Sheriff Holland that we had to leave. We'll be at the Lazy L ranch and would like him to come there.' He pressed a silver dollar into the old man's hand. 'That won't be enough maybe, but I'll make it up to you later.'

The old man nodded. 'It'll be all right, Luke. You go on about your business. I'll let the sheriff know come sun-up.'

It was full morning when the three pulled up at the hitch rack before Rube Lincoln's ranch house. He had heard the movement of their arrival and opened the door and walked out as Luke dismounted and turned to help a sleepy John Lucus from the saddle of his pony. Hannah sat in the saddle for some moments, weary from the fast ride and the lack of sleep. John Lucus was nearly asleep, and as Luke lifted him from the saddle, he yawned and asked where they were. Rube came around Hannah's mount and gave her a hand as she dismounted.

'Rube, there's trouble in the valley. My Indian *segundo* said that someone was running off my horses, and what cattle they could find. I need a change of horses, if you don't mind, and maybe a hand or two, if you can spare them.'

'Whatever I can do, I will, Luke, you know that. However, come in an' cookie will fix you some flapjacks an' eggs. With some black coffee that oughta make you feel better.'

86

Hannah spoke up. 'That sounds just right for us. Come on, John Lucus, let's get your face washed and after some breakfast, you'll be ready for anything.'

Luke nodded. 'Thanks, Rube. We needed that.' He turned to One Foot who had appeared from behind the house. 'After we eat, you stick around,' he said. 'We'll see what we can do.'

The Indian nodded. He gathered up the reins of the horses, moved off toward the corrals with them. Rube led the rest into the house and informed his cook that there were three more mouths to feed. The cook looked and seeing Luke and his family, grinned and nodded.

'I kin see about a dozen eggs, a steak and a pot of gravy disappearin' real fast, soon as I get it goin'. Warsh up, folks, I'll call when the vittles er ready.'

'Luke,' Rube brought a roughly drawn map to the table, now cleared of the breakfast meal. John Lucus was stretched out on a couch with a full belly, fast asleep. Hannah was sitting in a rocking chair before the fireplace, dozing. Luke and Rube remained at the table, and Rube spread the map before them. 'I got this after one of Sheridan's campaigns. It's about as good as we ever used in the Army. Here we are,' he pointed to the map. 'Now,' he moved his finger along the map, 'if them rustlers mean to take the hosses an' beef out over some lower pass, the closest railhead is here.' He thumped a blunt finger on a point. 'Fort Washakie.'

'What's there?' asked Luke. 'I've heard of it, but I've never been there.'

'It was a fort during some Indian uprisin's durin' a time before the Big War. But durin' the war, it was abandoned an' Indians pretty well destroyed it. Then the railroad come through an' made a junction there. Now it's used as a place to corral an' send beef, sold to a couple of middlemen there for big meat companies in the east. They take hosses, too, an' sell them to the army.'

Luke studied the map carefully. 'If I left here and drove hard, I could be there just about the time – maybe a little before – my rustled stock got there.' He raised his head and looked at Rube. Lincoln nodded.

'That was my thinkin',' he said. 'Me an' my boys will be glad to side you, since your crew is slightly short-handed.'

Luke still studied the map, then he nodded slowly.

'You are right. There is just one other thing. If you'll side me, like you said, I want Sheriff Holland to go along with us. We just might help him catch a rustler or two, and wring some information from them concerning the rest of the bunch.'

Lincoln nodded. 'I'll send a rider in for him. He can be here by noon an' we can leave right then.'

Hannah spoke up. 'Luke, I can't go on the trip with you, but John Lucus and I can go on to the ranch and wait for you there.'

Kane looked at her thoughtfully and then nodded slowly. 'I'll send One Foot with you. You'll be safe at the ranch with him and his nephews and their wives. I'll have One Foot have your horses ready by noon and you can leave for the ranch at the same time we leave for the fort. In the meantime, you stretch out somewhere and get some rest.'

It was mid afternoon before the sheriff arrived. He brought with him a deputy. A few minutes after his arrival the men left, led by Rube and Kane. With four men out of Lazy L crew, the sheriff and his deputy, Rube and Kane, there were eight of them. They were armed and ready to take on the rustlers at the railhead. Kane hoped to get there before the rustlers came up with the stolen beef and horses. He glanced at the sun as he mounted, after kissing Hannah goodbye and ordering his son to take care of his mother. He glanced at One Foot and the old Indian merely nodded. He would see that the woman and boy were taken safely to the ranch in the valley.

As they mounted, and led out of the ranch yards, Luke glanced at the sun and Rube spoke to him over the jingle of harness and slap of hoofs.

'It's a little late for us gettin' started,' he said, reining his mount close to that of Kane. 'But if we go on through the night, an' rest about midnight, we can be there just about daybreak. We just might be there afore the rustlers.'

Kane nodded. 'Let's ride,' he said.

SEVEN

Josh Carter was serious about getting the stolen animals to the railhead for shipment. He roused the cook out of his blankets at four in the morning, while it was still dark, and had him begin breakfast for the men. He kicked the boots of the wranglers, getting them up to prepare the *remuda* for the movement of cattle and horses over an ancient trail to the flats beyond the mountains. From that point to the railhead at old Fort Washakie would be a long day's drive. By sun-up he intended to be on the trail.

Jim Taylor stood drinking a second cup of scalding coffee and staring broodingly into the fire. Carter went up to him, and kneeling, poured himself a cup of coffee; then he stood looking at Taylor.

'What happened in Red Rock? You mean to tell me that Rob Ballard was slower than Luke Kane when it come to gettin' iron out of leather?'

Taylor sipped the brew again and shook his head. 'Nope. I didn't say that.'

'Then how come Rob was the one to hit the dust and not Kane?'

Taylor turned and looked at Carter, the firelight flickering red shadows on his face. 'Rob drawed first,' he said. 'I was standin' where I could see it all. He cleared leather and fired first. He missed. By the time he could ear back an' pull off another shot, that Kane turned slowly, an' levelin' his pistol like he was in a turkey shoot, his shot came the same time as Rob's second one, and drilled Rob right in the brisket.' He shook his head. 'That is the coolest man I ever did see in a gunfight.'

'You mean to tell me that Rob drawed first and fired first, an' still Kane got 'im first shot?'

Taylor nodded shortly. 'You must be hard of hearin', boss. That was what I just told you.'

Josh finished his coffee and tossed the dregs into the fire, where the moisture caused a hiss and a small flare-up. He shrugged and did not look at Taylor again. 'Get your beef rounded up an' ready to travel,' was all he said, and walked away.

Taylor watched him. There goes a coward, he thought. He wouldn't face Kane over pistols, for love or money. He finished his coffee and proceeded to rope his horse from the *remuda*, for the hard day's work of driving a herd of cattle through some very wild territory.

Carter left Taylor standing by the fire and motioned to two of his crew, who were finishing their meal. They came to him and he moved with them out of hearing distance of any of the rest of the men.

'I want you two to stay here. While we're

gone, I want you to scout out the Kane ranch headquarters. Just lay back in the hills and keep a glass on the place. I'm certain Kane's woman went into Red Rock with him. But I want to know, by the time I get back, if there's anyone left back there to look after things while Kane is gone.'

The men nodded and left to find their mounts. Carter moved to his bedroll and began preparing it for the trip to the railhead; blanket, tarp, piggin' strings, extra pistol and other possibles needed for such work. Then, he mused, when I get back, I'll be ready to make another ride on Kane's holdings. This time will get me what I want, Kane an' his holdin's an'... his woman!

Hannah and John Lucus with One Foot leading the way, left the Lazy L ranch a little after the departure of Kane on his way to reach the old fort before Carter appeared with the horses and cattle. Soon the ranch headquarters was hidden behind a rolling series of low hills, leading up to the mesa which drew a blue, ragged line across the foot of the mountains. Once Hannah paused and looked back. But the distance and the small cloud of dust, which she knew was caused by the posse, obscured any glimpse of horses and riders, let alone clear sighting of an individual, shadowing any yearning hope of a final glimpse of Luke Kane.

The passage way through the mesa wall brought memories of her first headlong trip here with Luke leading the way. As they came out of the narrowed crevice which opened on to a flat shelf overlooking the valley, she paused once again at the beauty of the land stretched out before her. Lush grazing for cattle and horses, flat areas for growing grain for their table and for the animals. A long, gentle sweep of the valley ending at the far end where sheer cliffs lifted into mountains yet unexplored. The wind was gentle and sky a blue vault above her, with a few tufted clouds floating, casting fleeting shadows upon the earth. And down there, beside the creek which seemed never to go dry, amongst the protection of a series of great pines and oak trees, was her home. Her home! Built with their hands, created with strain and sweat and some tears, but her home, their home.

John Lucus dismounted from his pony and came to stand beside her; he was silent for a long time; then he took her hand and looking up at her, he said, 'Come on, Mom, let's go home!'

Red Feather met them as they came out of the crevice, and followed them down to the house. There Black Hawk appeared from a tack shed and joined them on the broad front veranda. While One Foot and his nephews talked, Hannah entered the house, opened doors and windows, letting in fresh air, to push out the feeling of a house closed for a period of time. John Lucus, tired from the journey, went to his room to play, but was soon sleeping, stretched out on the carpet, one hand clutching a favorite familiar childhood toy.

The report given to One Foot was meager, but meaningful. The rustlers were gone, going out of the valley by a trail hard to traverse, but capable of passage. No one had tried to enter the valley through the opening in the valley wall. One Foot received the reports.

'Keep watching. I smell trouble for the valley,' he instructed the others.

It was approaching noon when Luke Kane and the posse drew up before the telegraph office in Fort Washakie. There were open corrals on the other side of the track, and ramps, used to load beef on to the cars.

There were no animals in the corrals. Kane nodded toward them.

'Looks like we got here in time,' he said to Rube Lincoln. He looked about him, seeing that there were only a few establishments. There was a saloon across the street from the telegraph office, next door to a building with a sign ROOMS & RESTRUNT. Beyond there was a merchandise store, which undoubtedly catered to the needs of those running the small businesses in the town. Luke noted that back of the main (and only) street were a few small houses. Homes for the few citizens of Fort Washakie.

Kane turned to Rube Lincoln.

'Why don't the boys go over and get a meal, while we wait. You and I, and the sheriff can go to the rooming-house and see if someone is there waiting to buy the herd when it gets here.'

Rube nodded, as did the sheriff. Rube spoke to the men.

'Go on an' get some vittles, boys, We'll join you at the saloon. Mind you now, only beer, until this shindig is over. Then we might tip a glass or two.' There was laughter and jeering, but all in good nature, as the men crossed the street to the restaurant and entered the door to the dining-area.

Luke led the way across the street to the rooming-house. The three of them entered the building, seeing only a sparsely furnished room, a few chairs, a horsehair divan to one side, and facing the door a small table behind which sat an elderly man, who watched them as they approached. The three of them lined up before the table and looked down at the man apparently in charge.

'Howdy,' he said, his keen eyes seeing the gleam of the sheriff's badge on his vest. 'What can I do for you? A room for you gentlemen?'

'Maybe,' said Luke. 'Is there a beef representative here, waiting for my herd to come in?'

'Well, there's a man here sayin' he's here to buy cattle, hosses an' whatever he can get, I reckon. I can roust him out fer you if it's real important.'

'Why don't you do just that,' said Luke. 'We'll wait right here until he comes.'

The man nodded. 'Just have seats, gents. I'll go get him.'

It was several minutes before the man returned, followed by a heavy-set, sweating individual, who showed the effects of being wakened and dressing hurriedly.

'These are the gents what wants to talk with you, Mr Willaby.' The man nodded to them and hurriedly drew up a chair across from Luke. Willaby's eyes were red-rimmed as though from the results of a long, sleepless night, or too many hours with John Barleycorn the evening before.

'What can I do for you gentlemen?' he rasped, clearing his throat several times.

Luke looked at Rube and met a shrug. He looked Willaby in the eyes and decided to lay it in his lap.

'You are waiting for a herd of beef, and some hosses?'

Willaby nodded, his eyes moving from one to the other. They lingered longer on the badge pinned to the vest of the sheriff. 'Well ... ah ... yes, yes, I do await a shipment which I believe will be arriving imminently. Why do you ask?'

'That herd belongs to me, Mr Willaby. You and I will have to palaver about it a bit before any agreement is reached,' said Luke, his voice cold.

'Ah ... I was to do business with a Mr Josh Carter, I do believe. Why is he not present? Is the herd coming in soon?'

'Mr Carter was unable to be with the herd

98

and sent us on ahead to meet with you,' Rube Lincoln said. 'Mr Kane, here, is in charge.'

'Oh ... well, that is different. You say you actually own the herd, Mr Kane?' The eyes were shrewd, narrowing as he turned his attention to Luke.

'Yes, I did not like the price Carter quoted to me,' he said solemnly. 'Just what did you promise him?'

Willaby hesitated and then cautiously replied, 'Ah, I do believe that I quoted him at eight dollars a head for the cattle, and fifteen to twenty dollars for each horse, according to how ready it was for the army.'

Luke looked at him, his eyes cold and his mouth drawn in a straight line. 'Mr Willaby, you are quoting to me prices you would give a rustler bringing you a stolen herd which you have to ship out in a hurry. I own the animals, I am in no hurry. Do you want to try again?'

Willaby grew red in the face. He blustered and then sighed. 'Well, I suspect I could go a bit higher, say ten dollars a head for the cattle and twenty to twenty-five for the horses. That is my absolute final bid.' He straightened his pudgy frame and attempted to look resolute in his offer. But his eyes shifted to the star on Holland's vest and he wiped his suddenly sweaty face with a handkerchief.

Luke shook his head and leaning forward held Willaby's eyes in a grim gaze. 'I am prepared to have the sheriff here arrest you for receiving stolen cattle and hosses. You will go to trial in our courts and they will send you away for dealing with rustlers – you may get anything from the rope to life in Yuma prison. That's where we send cattle- and hoss-thieves. Now, I will take twelve-fifty for the cattle and thirty for the hosses. No less. The sheriff here is ready to deal with you as aiding and abetting a rustling deal. The choice is yours.'

'You are robbing me!' screamed Willaby. He started to rise and the sheriff shoved him back into the chair.

'Let's hear your choice,' he said to Willaby. 'Mr Kane speaks true. You better accept his offer and let it go at that.'

Willaby seemed to wilt and then wiping his face again, he nodded.

'You have me between a rock and a hard place,' he admitted. 'I'll accept, but I want to see the head-count myself.

Luke rose and nodded. 'Meet us down at the corrals when the cattle arrive. We'll let you count along with me and Rube Lincoln here. The sheriff or his deputy will verify the count. When you hand over the money, I would suggest you get out of the territory as quick as a stage can take you. We don't like crooks like you hanging around. Someone might get careless with a forty-four in target practice and you'll be in the way.' The man paled and sweat again streaked his now chalky features. He nodded vigorously.

'I'll be there with the money, I'll be there!'

Luke, Rube and the sheriff went into the restaurant and ate a hurried meal. The sheriff sent his deputy out to watch for the incoming herd. When the men had finished with their dinner, Luke led them all to the barn beside the corrals.

'Keep out of sight,' Luke said to them. 'Let them push the herd into the corrals and then we'll let them know we are here.'

Sheriff Holland spoke. 'I want prisoners, boys. We'll let the law take care of them. But don't take any chances. If they show fight an' draw on you, let 'em have it. An' we especially want Carter an' whoever his foreman is.'

Luke looked at Rube. 'Where's that ranny, Taylor? I don't see him among the crew?'

Rube looked at him with a puzzled expression on his face. 'He wasn't around when I got the crew together,' he said. 'That's strange.'

Luke nodded. 'Maybe,' he said. 'I saw Taylor jawing with that Ballard character who drawed on me. Maybe Taylor was in with this gang, and using the Lazy L as a hideout and a place to spy on the law and them of us which try to support it.'

Rube's face grew grim. 'I think you may be right. He's fair game, same as all of them.'

The deputy was in the barn loft, watching the hills behind the town, the direction from which the herd had to come. Luke spread the men out over the barn, ready to move at the report of the stolen herd approaching.

There was no movement among those waiting and watching. Some seemed tense, but as the time wore on, they relaxed. The liveryman came from dinner and stood surprised and bug-eyed at all the armed men standing along the walls of the barn. Luke motioned him to come over.

'That herd coming in soon is rustled stock.' He nodded to the sheriff. The man turned and caught a glimpse of the star on Holland's vest. He gulped and nodded quickly.

'S'all right with me, boss,' he said. 'I'll just go back to the saloon an' wait 'til it's all over.'

'You do that, and have a beer on me,' Luke told him. 'And be quiet about what's going on here.'

'Silent as a rock, mister.' The old man turned and disappeared through the big front door of the barn, into the sunlight of the barn lot. He had hardly had time to get to the saloon when the deputy called down from the hayloft. 'Sheriff, there's a herd comin' in. Looks like about eight fellers pushin' it.'

'That's them,' Luke said. 'Now, wait until the herd is in the corrals and then we'll slip out and have a talk with the drivers.'

Luke and Rube, with the sheriff, crowded into an empty stall where there was a small window that opened out upon the side which the herd was approaching. Luke could see the cattle being pushed in front, with the small bunch of half-broken horses being hazed along back of them, to one side, out of the drift of the dust cloud raised by the hooves.

The men in the barn watched through cracks in the wall, and waited. The herd was driven into the corral, pushed in by yells and slapping rope ends. The horses were driven to another corral on the far side of the barn away from the cattle.

When the last corral gate was closed, Luke spoke to his crew. 'All right, boys, let's go give them a polite welcome.'

The sheriff said grimly, 'I want Carter and Taylor if no one else.'

EIGHT

Josh Carter was with the horse herd to one side of the cattle with its dust and heat. Jim Taylor was on point, leading the herd to the corrals. As Taylor turned to direct the leaders of the herd to the corral openings, he pulled up on his reins. Something was wrong.

The town was still. There were no by-standers on the boardwalks watching the herd come in. There were no youngsters chasing dogs and throwing rocks and sticks, playing in the main street, as would be usual. Things were too quiet. Wary, he moved back, keeping the herd between himself and the barn.

As the last of the cattle were hazed into the corrals, the quietness burst into a cacophony of yells, cursing and then shots being fired. Seeing the group of men erupting from the barn, bearing six-guns and rifles, Taylor drew his Colt .44 and leveled a shot at one of the men closest to him. The man ducked, and rolling, came up shooting. Taylor heard the bullets whistling about his ears and decided this was not where he ought to be. He whirled his horse around to leave and as he did so he saw Luke Kane leading two men around the cattle corrals to where the horses had been driven into their own holding place. He fired a quick shot at Kane and as the man paused, looked and located him, leveling his gun, Taylor laid low over his horse and gave it the spurs.

The fire-fight was going fiercely. Carter's men crouched behind posts, watering troughs, crouching on the ground, wherever cover might offer itself, and were firing at Rube Lincoln and the crew. Here and there a yell of pain rose as a slug found a target.

Josh Carter knew somehow his scheme for selling the cattle and horses for depriving Paradise Valley and its owner, Luke Kane of his livelihood, had fallen apart. Then he saw

Rube Lincoln and Kane running around the near side of the horse corral, coming directly toward him. They had seen him!

Cursing, he whirled his mount again, drawing his pistol and hurriedly firing at the two running men. He did not linger to see if his shots were any way effective, but gigged his horse cruelly with sharp spurs and raced away from the turmoil that was erupting around the barn and corrals. He knew it was over for him, and that if he was caught, it would be the rope, or lifetime imprisonment, to say the least.

Kane yelled and fired at the racing leader of the outlaw gang, wishing he had brought along his rifle. But, seeing the leader of the gang escaping, he turned his attention to the action nearby. The sheriff and his deputy had organized the men well, and now, surrounded, Carter's men were giving up, coming from their hiding places with arms high and tossing their weapons to the ground. One of them was dead, two more were wounded. And all were aware that hard times lay before them, as the grim-faced sheriff rounded them up and began to bind the arms of each man with pigging strings, tying them to their saddle horns, as they were pushed into the saddles they had abandoned so hurriedly.

Kane and Lincoln came up, herding three of the gang before them, their hands tied behind their backs.

'Carter an' Taylor got away,' the sheriff told them grimly. 'But some of these rannies will sing like nightingales an' give us details about their actions of the past few months. We'll get Carter an' Taylor before it's all over.'

Rube Lincoln shook his head and rubbed his bearded chin. 'I just can't see how I didn't catch on to that Taylor. He used me, an' I ain't forgettin' that. No man uses me an' gets away with it.'

'Don't feel bad about it,' Kane said to him. 'He's a pretty slick character, and it's hard for an honest man to see what he really is until something like this springs up. We'll get him and he'll wish he had never heard of the Lazy L.'

He stood in the shadowed doorway of the mercantile store and watched the fight around the corrals. His sharp eyes missed nothing. He saw Luke Kane placing his men, and leading them against the rustlers and a thin smile crossed his lips. Kane was still the fighter he had known him to be during the war years when they both served for a short while with General Joe Selby, but then had moved on to fight in separate battles for the South. Ben Thompson had a date with destiny in the near future, but at the moment he was interested in one Jim Taylor.

He had followed Taylor out of Texas, through the Colorado Territory and had finally received word that the man was working for a ranch in the Wyoming Territory. In Red Rock he had learned through saloon gossip that Taylor was now riding with an owl-hoot gang, led by Josh Carter. Thompson's lip curled slightly. He had met up with Carter briefly over a game of five-card stud. Carter was a weak, cheating excuse for a man in Thompson's opinion and it did not surprise him that the man he sought would be involved with such a person.

Now he knew pretty well where Taylor would be. He would find him. In the meantime it looked as though his old army acquaintance might need a hand. Thompson narrowed his gaze. Then he saw Taylor was following another plume of dust, created by an escaping rustler. Thompson surmised it to be Carter, who could take off for far places when it appeared he was on the end of a short rope. Thompson nodded to himself and watched as Rube Lincoln and Kane left the corrals and walked toward the rooming-house.☙

The Eastern beef representative came hurrying down the rooming-house stairs carrying two bags and a valise under one arm. He slid to a stop and paled, as he stood face to face with Luke Kane and Rube Lincoln.

'I ... ah ... I was just coming to look for you. We can make a head count of the cattle now, and then I will be on my way.'

'You look like you're in a big hurry to go somewhere?' said Rube, dryly.

'Oh ... ah ... yes, the stage is due in any minute now–'

'Stage won't be in fer a hour or so,' interjected the rooming-house owner and clerk. 'Anyway, he has to change teams, let the passengers rest a mite, an' get him a drink of whiskey afore he starts out agin. I reckon he'll be here plenty time fer you to make your head count an' give these gents their money. How come the stage an' not the train?'

Willaby's face turned red and then paled

109

as he stared into Luke Kane's cold eyes.

'The train bypasses my next place to visit. However, I believe there is time for this business.'

'Uh-huh,' said Kane. 'I reckon you were goin' to set outside in the sun 'til the stage comes along. Well, Mr Willaby, you can come with us and make a headcount, or you can take our count, which by the way, has been verified by the sheriff. It's up to you, but time's awastin'.'

It was a disgruntled Willaby who followed Kane to the corrals and there, perched on a corral pole with a pencil and paper, made the count of the cattle and then the horses. It was an hour later when he sighed and reached into his inner jacket pocket and pulled out a bulging wallet.

'I was prepared to give Mr Carter a check on the company bank in Chicago. I presume that will be sufficient for–'

'Nope,' said Kane. 'You were not giving Carter a check. Where could he go cash it, him being a wanted man? You was ready to pay him cash. That's what I want.'

Willaby wilted. 'You are a harsh man, Mr Kane. I don't know if I have enough–'

'You have enough. You had it for Carter, you have it for us. Now start counting.'

Slowly Willaby opened the wallet. 'Let me see, that was ten and half for cattle and twenty-five for horses.'

Kane shook his head. 'Your hearing ain't so good, and my patience is running out. Twelve-fifty for the cattle per head, and thirty-five for twenty-one horses and mares. That comes to four thousand four hundred eighty-three dollars total. Now you just count it out in our hands and Rube, here, and I will be able to tote it back to my bank in Red Rock.'

Begrudgingly opening the valise, Willaby counted out the amount owed, filling Lane's hands with one hundred and fifty-dollar bills. Finished, he snapped the valise shut and glared at them.

'You cost me money on this deal, and I'll never forget it!'

'Naw, we didn't cost you nothin',' said Rube wryly. 'You just ain't gettin' as much as you planned fer yourself. Your company had better maybe watch you closer, you're gettin' rich off them.'

Kane and Rube left him and went to the barn where the sheriff had his prisoners mounted and ready to go, with Rube's crew surrounding them. It would be two long days to Red Rock and jail for the rustlers.

Ben Thompson watched Kane and the crew leaving. He had heard enough to know that they were headed to Red Rock, and that Kane had no real crew running his ranch in the mountains. He decided he would approach Kane at the Lazy L ranch, for it was reasonable that Kane would accompany his friend, the owner of the ranch, on his way back into the mountains and his ranch, wherever it might be. Thompson surmised that there would be further trouble with Carter and Taylor, and by attaching himself to Kane, he would have the opportunity he desired to confront Taylor, whom he wanted.

Leaving shortly after Kane and Lincoln led their crew out of Fort Washakie, he took a longer way around, cutting through some rough country where Kane would not wish to lead his group of prisoners and the posse, riding swiftly and stopping to rest his horse only occasionally, gnawing on hard dried biscuits and some jerky, he was in Red Rock several hours before Kane. A couple of questions for directions and he rode on to the Lazy L, there to wait until Rube Lincoln came in with his crew, sure that Luke Kane would be with them.

NINE

Black Hawk came reporting to One Foot that there were two men left in the campsite he had been watching. Everyone else was gone with the cattle and horses.

'My woman needs meat for the lodge,' he told his uncle. 'I will go hunting. Red Feather is still watching the valley door. The woman will be safe with you here and with no one able to come in without being seen.'

One Foot was thoughtful. He was uneasy that the two men left at the outlaw camp were not under surveillance, yet he knew what it was to have no meat for the fire, and a woman could provide everything but the meat. Finally he nodded.

'Go bring some meat. Bring enough for Red Feather and for my lodge. Do not take long. We need to know what those two men are doing all the time.'

One Foot was correct. The action of the two men needed constant watch. Now they were free to go where and do whatever they wished. This troubled him.

It was two nights after Black Hawk's departure to hunt. Hannah and John Lucus had sat on the porch for several hours, watching the stars and wondering how long it would be before Luke came home. They went to bed at last, and settled in for the night. Before she went to her room, Hannah left the porch and approached a huge live-oak tree a few feet from the porch. One Foot rose from the dark shadows and awaited her approach

'We are going to bed, One Foot, is everything all right?'

The Indian nodded stoically. 'Quiet, Miss Hannah. Red Feather watches gate. Black Hawk hunting. I watch the house and all.'

She shivered and hugged herself. The air was cool, but not cold. Some inward impulse sent a shiver through her.

'I wish Luke was here. I worry about him.'

The old Indian eyed her, his eyes glittering in some wayward star gleam.

'You no worry, Miss Hannah. Luke Kane a man. He will be here soon. He will be all right.'

She nodded in the darkness. 'I know, but it doesn't keep me from worrying.' She shook herself, as if to cast off her feelings. 'I feel

114

safe with you watching, my friend.'

She bade him goodnight and entered the house again. Unsettled, she wandered about, touching this table and that shelf, seeing Luke's things, wishing for him. Wanting him to hold her close, to take her to bed and comfort her. She sighed. Why was she feeling so empty, so unsettled, she mused. She was not this kind of a woman to become upset over something she knew was all right. He would be here, he was safe.

She checked on John Lucus, finding him sleeping soundly, one hand outside the quilt, clutching his favorite beaver cap made for him by Black Hawk's woman, who doted upon him. She smoothed his hair, pulled the quilt a little further up on his shoulders and smiled. Softly she bent over and kissed his forehead and rising, went to her room, leaving the door to her son's room open so she might hear any unusual stir or commotion.

She slept finally, deeply and soundly, undreaming until—

Milo Swartz and Buck Leonard had stayed behind on Carter's orders. He left them with a specific instruction. 'If the way is clear an' you can pull it off, get Kane's woman an' bring her here with the young 'un. Once I have her, I'll have him over a barrel an' he'll sign anything to get them back safe, even turn the deed of his spread over to me.' He smirked at them. 'An' keep your hands off the woman. She's my property, understand?'

Swartz and Leonard watched the Kane homestead. They saw Hannah and John Lucus return and get settled into the house, following their trip into Red Rock. The first day after their return the two men saw Black Hawk leave with a pack mule and rifle and surmised correctly that the Indian would be away several hours on a hunting trip. They did not see Red Feather, and did not know of his presence, however they did watch One Foot as he worked about the corrals and sheds. It was their opinion that the Indian was guarding the woman and boy until Luke Kane returned.

On the evening of Hannah's second day home, clouds rolled in across the mountains and after sundown the landscape was shrouded in darkness. A light rain began to fall and Swartz and Leonard decided it would be a good time to get the woman and boy from the house and back to the campsite. They expected Carter and Taylor to ride in sometime during the night.

The rain softened the ground and their approach was silent as they came up to the corrals of the Kane holdings. There were no lights in the house. They were certain that the Indian was somewhere about, and Swartz, being the best at movement in such circumstances, reconnoitered the nearby sheds and house.

One Foot would forever after be completely chagrined, shamed in fact, that he had dozed off in his place beneath the huge old live-oak tree, at the end of the front porch of the house. Alertness had forever been part of his character, his life. Hundreds of times during his years he had spied upon white soldiers during the Indian wars, almost under their feet, and kept awake for days and nights. But for Indian as well as any human, age had dulled his perceptions, his bones ached from countless nights lying on hard ground, senses lessened with the passing years, and One Foot, once the ever alert Indian, dozed in the warmth of the evening and deep shadows of the tree. He stirred slightly when the rain began, but drew a blanket over his shoulders and dozed off again.

Swartz found him thus. He knocked him

unconscious and tied him with a short piece of rope which he carried at all times. He gagged One Foot with the Indian's bandanna and rolled him deeper under the tree. The Indian would be unconscious long enough for Swartz and Leonard to do what they had come to do.

The men entered the house quietly. The heavy front door was not latched. There was one lamp burning on a low wick, giving off a pale yellow gleam. Inside the door they waited and listened. Swartz looked around and surveyed the layout of the house. The bedrooms lay off a short hall. Motioning for Leonard to follow, he slipped silently down the hall. Peering into one room he saw the boy sleeping and nudged Leonard.

'Go in an' grab the young 'un. Don't hurt him, just scare the pants off him an' bring him into the next bedroom.'

Leonard nodded and Swartz moved on. He stood for a long moment in the doorway of the bedroom. Hannah was in the bed. Turning in her sleep, her gown was open several buttons and Swartz was tempted to throw himself upon her. He resisted, however, thinking that the time would come later. Moving swiftly to the bed, he leaned down and, grabbing her head with one hand, slapped a rough palm over her mouth.

Hannah snapped awake and threw herself away from the man, seizing with both hands the paw over her face. But he was big and strong, and he jerked her back into the bed and turned her so she could see the door.

'Now you be quiet an' good, or you'll see what will happen to the boy!'

Leonard moved in from the hall and Hannah gasped in fear, as she saw John Lucus held in the outlaw's hands, his eyes wide and staring with fright. Leonard pressed a cocked pistol at the boy's head.

'Now, you do what we say an' the young 'un won't be hurt,' Swartz growled at her. 'We're both wanted men, the rope or prison facing us, if we're caught. So another killin' or two won't make no difference.'

Hannah nodded, her eyes filling with tears as she saw the white, frightened face of her son. Swartz removed his hand from her mouth. 'Don't make a sound,' he warned, 'or you'll find you're a ma without a kid. Now, get some rain gear together for both of you. I don't want my boss, who I'm takin' you to, yellin' at me 'cause you get sick from the storm. Now, get movin'.'

He sat on the side of the bed while Hannah, moving numbly, gathered up a poncho and a man's hat. Followed by John Lucus and Leonard, she went to her son's room and dropped a smaller poncho over his head and shoulders, and gave him a hat. He clutched his beaver-skin cap and refused the hat. She shrugged and looked at Swartz.

'Let me put on a pair of boots.'

He shrugged and followed her into the room. Taking his attention from her for a second, looking about the spacious bedroom, he did not see her slip a small derringer into her boot-top.

'You ready now? Let's go.' He motioned to Leonard. 'Go out to the corral an' rope a hoss for them to ride. I'll bring them there an' we'll be on the road, storm or not.'

Hannah wondered where Black Hawk and One Foot could be. She had left the old Indian under the big tree just beyond the porch. But as Swartz shoved them past the tree, she could not see into the shadows enough to know if One Foot was still there. She had a chilling thought. The only way they could have gotten into the house was by killing the old Indian. Her heart clutched at the thought. He had been with them for most of the time they were developing Paradise Valley ranch.

Leonard had the horse ready. Hannah

mounted and Swartz lifted John Lucus to the cantle behind the saddle. The boy put his arms about his mother's waist, and hugged her tightly. A deeply frightened little boy, he still did not cry or protest. He seemed to realize that they were in danger, and that he must depend upon his mother to set the example of their compliance. He thought, stoutly, that his father would ultimately rescue them.

Swartz led out, and with Hannah's mount following him, Leonard dropped in behind them, allowing no opportunity for them to escape into the darkness of the storm. Within minutes of their leaving the house, they were feeling the dampness creeping into their ponchos, dripping down the backs of their necks. She felt her son shiver and knew that he was being affected by the storm. And the storm deepened. Rain lashed at them and wind pushed against them, the horses laboring through the strength of nature's surliness. Suddenly Hannah had a heart-rending thought. The storm would wash away all tracks, all indication of direction. Even One Foot, great tracker that he was, would not be able to read the signs. Depression filled her and she wept silently and deeply. Where were they taking her? What was the purpose? Her, perhaps, but why John Lucus, a small, innocent boy? But deep down, she knew the purpose. This was Josh Carter's evilness at work. Hating both her and Kane, he had some diabolical scheme in mind.

Feeling the boy shivering, she stopped her horse. Leonard came up beside her and cursed, yelling at her in the howling darkness, his voice whipped away by the wind. Hannah ignored him and dismounted. Swartz rode back and yelled at her, but she stubbornly ignored both of them. She unrolled a blanket she had placed behind the saddle, with no argument from Swartz. She wrapped it about her son and moved him into the saddle before her. Remounting, she wrapped her arms about him, burying him in the blanket. Swartz nodded, and started out again, with Leonard, growling and irritable, coming behind. She did not speak during the interlude. They plodded on through the storm, in the darkness of night, only Swartz seeming to know the direction and where they were going.

It was growing light when finally the three arrived at Carter's campsite. Hannah had no idea where they were. She had never been to this part of the valley. She dismounted stiffly and reaching up, lifted John Lucus to the ground. She glanced about. There were signs of camping, fire-blackened stones about a firehole, dried logs and limbs piled about for fuel. It all indicated to her that Carter and his gang had been camped here for some time. She looked at Swartz who had returned from putting the horses in a roped-off corral.

'Now what?' she asked.

He shrugged. 'Come with us.'

Motioning for them to follow, he walked away from the campsite up a short slope, and down a coulee that deepened as they entered. He stopped before a slight rise and led them to a flattened area about twenty feet from the coulee floor. He bent over, pulled some loose brush aside and disclosed a wide hole in the face of the cliff. He rose and motioned to the hole.

'This is a little cave. Carter said to put you in there until he comes. It's safe and I'll build a fire for you. You can light torches from the fire for more light.' He motioned to Leonard. 'Go on in an' make sure there's no varmint hidin' in there.'

Leonard glared at him and backed away.

'Go in yourself,' he snapped. 'I ain't goin'

in no hole like that. Thar might be rattle-snakes or even a bear.' Swartz looked at him and shook his head.

'You are something of a brave man, Buck,' he said. Seizing a handful of sagebrush, he twisted it and then lighted it with a match. 'Watch them,' he smirked at Buck. 'That boy there just might overpower you an' take your gun.' Bending, he held the torch before him and entered the cave. Leonard frowned at John Lucus and the boy stared back at him boldly. Hannah moved over in front of the boy and looked levelly at Leonard.

'You don't frighten us,' she told him. 'Carter wants us for some reason and you won't buck him, I'm sure. Now leave us alone.'

Swartz appeared from the cave mouth at that time. 'You can come in,' he said, 'there's no varmints. An' there's wood there, enough to make a fire.' He glanced at Buck. 'Why don't you stand guard an' shoot any var-mints that I might have missed.' He grinned and winked arrogantly at Leonard.

Hannah knew there was no use arguing with the men. This was what Carter had ordered and he was boss. If she fought them they would probably tie both her and John Lucus and toss them into the cave regardless. She motioned for her son to follow her, and bending, entered the cave. John Lucus, wide-eyed and hanging on to her poncho, was followed by Swartz.

As the rustler had said, there was wood for a fire. She gathered some into a pile and Swartz lighted it from another torch he had made. The dry wood caught fire and soon a small blaze worked its way through the smaller pieces of wood and the larger ones began to burn. Swartz looked at her.

'Miz Kane, I don't want you or the boy to suffer. Carter pays me – sometimes – an' I'm the kind that follows such as him. But I don't fight women an' children. I won't let him hurt you while I'm around. So, make the best of this you can. I 'spect it'll come out all right sooner or later.' He nodded and left the cave.

Hannah looked about her. She pulled John Lucus close to her and wrapped her arms about him, both of them warmed by the blanket and by the fire which was growing larger all the time. She noticed writing on the walls and realized that this had at one time or another been used by Indians. The room was fairly large, and she noted that the smoke from the fire drifted toward the back of the room. Perhaps a tunnel led off in that direction, she thought. She leaned over and placed another piece of wood on the fire. Tears flowed down her cheeks. Where was Luke? Why was Carter taking his hatred out on her and the boy who had done him no wrong? Oh, she had repulsed him a few times when married to his cousin, Bruce Carter, the former sheriff of the county. But that was over ten years ago. Could dislike or hatred last so long?

She held her son close to her and drew the blanket tighter about them, gazing into the fire. Fear clutched her heart and she wept; a woman strong in so many ways, she was at the end of her strength, physically and mentally. The future looked to her as black as the cave beyond the flickering blaze of the small fire.

TEN

Ben Thompson, one-time dandy, given to silk hats and fancy clothes, part-time gunman, sometime lawman and generally badman, was waiting on the porch of Rube Lincoln's house when Lincoln and Luke

Kane arrived. The horses were turned over to two of the men who were with them, and the spread-owner and Kane walked up to the porch, slapping dust from their chaps.

Kane halted and looked at Thompson who had risen as they approached. He eyed the man, recognizing him with a grimace. Thompson was not nor had he ever been one of Luke's favorite people. Rube Lincoln was not acquainted with Thompson and looked at him questioningly.

'Howdy,' he said. 'I reckon I don't know you. But I guess you know me, or about my spread, or you'd not be here.'

'This is Ben Thompson,' Luke said to him, eyeing Thompson. 'How you been, Thompson?'

'Tolerable, just tolerable,' said Thompson laconically. 'Heard you had a little run in with rustlers.'

Luke nodded. 'Nothing we couldn't handle.' He looked at Thompson quizzically. 'The last I heard of you, you'd joined up with General Selby and was on the way to Mexico with him and his crew.'

Thompson nodded. 'I pulled out when I found out he was serious about it. I've been to a lot of places and done a lot of things since that time with Selby. You was with him, too, for a while, wasn't you?'

Luke nodded. 'You and I both was with him during the Arkansas campaign. But I got tired of his method of fighting the war. I pulled out and went east and was in most of the battles, Shiloh, Nashville, Chickamauga. I was at Appomattox and saw Bobby Lee ride away on his white horse. When he quit so did I. I come back and joined the Texas Rangers.'

Thompson looked broodingly in the distance, seeing the hazy blue line of the mesa. 'I got tired of it all, too.'

Rube Lincoln rose. 'How about a bite to eat? I know Luke here wants to get on the way to his spread beyond the mesa. I'll have cookie put on a couple more plates.'

Luke nodded. 'That's kindly of you, Rube. After I eat I'll go to the line shack on the mesa. That'll put me in the valley by noon tomorrow.'

Thompson looked at Luke. 'Did I see Carter skedaddlin' high-tail away from you and your posse back there yesterday?'

'He was there and he ran,' Luke said coldly. 'He's twice a rustler at least, and he's also broke prison. I ain't seen no flyer on him being wanted, but I suspect he's a wanted man by the law. I *know* he's a wanted man – by me!'

Thompson nodded shortly. 'He's teamed up with Jim Taylor, too. I saw both of them taking off after the fight started. I want to face either or both of them.' He looked closely at Kane. 'I'd appreciate it if you wouldn't mind my tagging along with you. I think they're after you for some reason, an' that would be the easiest way for me to get them to gun range.'

Luke eyed him for a long moment, searching his face. He knew Ben Thompson. Usually just a step before the law. Usually in some trouble. Always a magnet to gunfighters who wished to cut his notch on their guns. He did not particularly like the man. But he understood Thompson's drive to come up to the two men he mentioned. Luke hoped to corner them, too, to turn them over to the law.

He nodded. 'You are welcome to come with me. Just remember that first and foremost I want Carter and his rustlers cornered and captured. I want as little bloodshed as possible, but with these owl-hoot riders, I reckon they will fight it out. Better that, than prison. And they know if we turn them over to the sheriff, it will be the rope or prison, according to the judge and jury.'

'Fine by me,' Thompson said.

After taking time for a good meal, prepared by Lincoln's range cook, Kane and Thompson left the Lazy L spread and headed for the blue line of the mesa. It was full dark when they arrived at the line shack in which Kane had spent many days when a line-rider for the Lazy L, corralling and caring for their horses. They entered the shack, clearing it of two frightened pack-rats and a bird that had made its nest in the rafters.

Luke built a small fire outside the cabin in a ring of stones where there were signs of other camp-fires having been lighted. Over an iron grill he had brought to the shack years before, four big steaks were sizzling, with potatoes baking in the ashes. A pot of coffee heated and then simmered at the edge of the fire.

With a good meal under their belts, several cups of coffee enjoyed, and the after-meal smoke, they rolled up in their blankets and, with saddles as pillows, were soon asleep. There were night sounds, birds chirping sleepily, an owl complained in the distance – these sounds Kane heard and identified. Not far away came the low cough of a mountain lion, but the wary animal scented the presence of humans, and gave the line shack and its occupants a wide berth.

Kane had them up and moving at first light, and by noon he had led Thompson out of the slit through the mesa face. Then he paused. The figure of Red Feather appeared silently before them. Thompson drew back his horse sharply on seeing the Indian. His face darkened and his hand slapped against he butt of his sixgun. Kane grabbed his hand and held it steady.

'He's my Indian guard, and rider when needed.' He looked at Red Feather and nodded. 'This is Ben Thompson. He's visiting with us for a while.

Red Feather stared hard into Kane's eyes. 'Bad things happen, Kane. You go talk with my uncle at the house. Bad things.'

Kane looked grimly at him. 'My wife and boy, are they all right?'

Red Feather did not change expression. 'Bad. You go talk with my uncle.'

Without further comment, Luke motioned to Thompson and led the way off the shelf in front of the entrance to the valley. He did not pause to enjoy the panorama spread before him, but grimly set off on a trail made by himself and the Indians over the years.

Thompson saw the house, low and spreading beneath the live-oaks and huge pines. He sensed something was very wrong and did not speak. Kane was a cold, stolid, unemotional figure leading him down the long slope. In a few minutes they drew up before the corral and Black Hawk came out to get their horses. He nodded stoically to Kane, gave Thompson a keen, black-eyed glance and then nodded toward the house. 'Uncle there,' he said. He took the reins of the horses and led them away.

Kane turned and, carrying his saddle-bags, strode up the path to the porch. He looked up and saw One Foot standing, waiting. He stopped and Thompson stayed back of him, waiting for whatever would transpire between the Indian and Kane.

'Where are my wife and son?' Kane asked One Foot, softly, a knife edge in his voice. 'Where are they?'

One Foot's stoic expression did not change. His lips moved and the words came softly. He held Kane's eyes steadily with his own gaze.

'Wife and boy gone. Taken, what is your word – kidnapped?'

Kane's eyes burned as he heard the words. The sounds of the world shut out and his head whirled in a sudden dizziness. Gone?

'Where?' he asked, sinking on to the step below the Indian.

'Not know,' said One Foot. 'No tracks. Looked but not find.' He shrugged and made a gesture toward the valley. 'Somewhere out there.'

ELEVEN

Somehow Hannah fell asleep, with John Lucus held tightly against her, both wrapped in the blanket.

She awoke suddenly at a slight noise. The fire in the circle of stones was nearly out, there was just a faint glow of coals still hot. She noted this and stirred to place more wood upon the fire. The noise came again. Shivers of fear ran through her and she sat up, sliding the boy on to the ground behind her, and covering him with the blanket.

She placed some small pieces of wood on the embers and a bright flame fingered up among the pieces. The noise again ... and Buck Leonard loomed up out of the shadows. She started and moved back until she was against the body of the boy. He stirred and muttered and did not waken.

'What do you want? Why are you here?' She kept her voice low, hoping not to awaken John Lucus.

Buck stepped closer to the fire, and in the dim light of the flames, now burning well, she saw his smirk. 'Why, Miz Kane, I come to offer you comfort an' company.' He leered at her. 'I even brung you another blanket, see?' He took the rolled-up blanket from under his arm and tossed it across the fire to her. She seized it and thrust it aside, her eyes never leaving his face.

'You never did anything kind to any living creature, Buck Leonard,' she told him coolly. 'Now get out of here and leave us alone. You've done enough to us as it is.'

'Aw, now, Miz Kane. I'm just a ordinary man who likes to look at a purty woman. An' right now, you're the purtiest one in this camp.'

'Then go find one prettier than I,' she retorted. But Leonard, tiring of the talking, eased himself around the fire toward her.

'I come to get you, an' that's what I aim to do. Now, just be easy an' that's the way it's goin' to be. Just move away from the kid an' I'll be real easy with you.' With that he moved quickly to close the distance between them. As he reached for her, Hannah reached into her boot top and the small derringer appeared in her hand, the firelight gleaming off its metal frame. Leonard stopped in mid stride.

'Now, woman, where'd you hide that purty little pop-gun? Ain't you the clever one. Well, first place, you ain't gonna shoot me, right in front of your son. An' second, that little thing wouldn't hurt a fly.'

'Make one more step toward us, Leonard, and you will find out whether it will sting or not. And I know how to handle a weapon. Now, you just back away and leave the cave. Where is Mr Swartz, anyhow? He said he would see that we were not bothered until your boss, Josh Carter, arrived?'

Leonard was silent, eyeing the weapon, wondering whether this woman thought enough of her virtue to shoot a man. 'Swartz is out looking fer a hoss that wandered off,' he muttered. 'An' Carter won't be here fer another day maybe. So, just put down the gun, honey, an' everything will be all right.' He stepped closer. Raising the derringer, Hannah fired. The little weapon blasted with a fury unsuspected, and a .32 caliber bullet smashed into Leonard's chest.

He grunted and stepped back, looking down at the blood that was beginning to discolor his vest.

'Why you little...' he cursed and reached for her. John Lucus fought his way out of the blanket and rolled back into the darkness. Hannah ducked Leonard's grasp and rose to her knees. He seized her by the shoulders and attempted to shove her to the ground. She cocked the small weapon again and as his arms closed about her, she pushed the derringer into his belly and pulled the trigger. The shot was muffled between their bodies, but he grunted and rolled away from her. He rose to his knees and clutched his stomach.

'Why ... woman, you've kilt me.' His eyes glazed and he clutched his belly just above the belt buckle where the slug had entered his intestines and torn its way through vital organs. He staggered to his feet, turned and fell face down in the dust of the cavern floor.

Hannah whirled and clutching John Lucus to her, hid his face against her body.

'Is ... is he dead?' John Lucus asked, shakily.

Hannah rocked him and kissed his forehead. 'I think so,' she said. 'But if he isn't it will be a long time before he bothers anyone else.' However, she need not have worried. Buck Leonard was dead. As she pondered upon what she had done, she shivered at the thought of what Josh Carter might do to her at the killing of one of his men.

She noticed that the fire was almost out again, but suddenly there was light in the room. She looked toward the entrance of the cave, thinking Swartz or some other was entering the cave. She moved her eyes away from the entrance and away from the body of Leonard and looked toward the back of the cave.

She saw him and screamed!

He was old. He was dressed in Indian garb such as she had never seen, and as a Western woman, she had come into contact with members of several tribes. But this man was old. His eyes were buried deep in his leathery face. The hair was grey and pulled back in a ponytail and tied with a cloth or leather cord. He stood in the mouth of the tunnel which led away from the main room of the cavern. A light shone about him, soft and mellow, and then she noticed that his face was kind, his eyes searching her face. He turned his eyes to John Lucus and

137

strangely enough, the boy did not appear to fear the man or apparition, whatever it might be. Instead he looked at the Indian and asked, 'Is he real?'

Hannah was frightened, yet somehow realized that the Indian, or whatever it was, was not harmful.

'I don't know,' she answered him. 'He is strange.'

Strange indeed, she thought. Am I dreaming? Is this some form of dream, wishing for rescue by *something*, whatever it might be. She shook her head and the figure was the same, looking at her solemnly, but kindly. Then it spoke, gesturing with one hand.

'Do not be afraid,' it said. She was surprised to hear it speak in her own language. Spanish she could understand very well and converse in it. But no Indian language with the exception of a few words taught her by Black Hawk's wife, who worked with her in the big house, keeping it clean and helping her with cooking.

'You are in much danger here,' the Indian continued, slowly, watching her face. 'Bad men have brought you here and will be very bad with you, when they return.' He pointed slowly to the body of Leonard. 'You are a brave, strong woman. Come. I will show you a room only my people ever knew existed.'

'Who are your people?' John Lucus spoke up. 'What kind of Indian are you? I never saw one with clothes like yours.'

The lips of the Indian moved in a slight smile. 'You are a brave boy, strong boy. You will make a fine warrior.' He eyed John Lucus carefully. 'I am called The Old One. But they are wrong. I am older than the Old Ones they talk about. You call them *Anasazi*. But my people were older than they. This cave and many like them were our homes. The wall writings are ours. A few of us walk, partly in the spirit world, partly as you see me. I will help you, take you where the bad men will not find you. When they are gone, I will show you how to return to your home.'

Hannah relaxed. She was still frightened, but this man, spirit, person or dream made sense to her.

'I believe you,' she told the Old One. 'I am afraid of the men who brought us here. I trust what you offer.' Taking the blanket Leonard had thrown to her, she spread it over the body of its former owner. She replaced the derringer in her boot-top and taking John Lucus by the hand, she looked at the Indian.

'We are ready. I trust you.'

The Indian looked at her for a long moment and then gestured for them to follow him. He held no torch. A dim light shone about him, making it possible to see enough to follow him, and to keep from stumbling on unaccustomed footing. He led into a tunnel leading off the back of the cave and a little further on slipped into a crevice in the wall. It was narrow and dank, but the man moved forward, gesturing again for them to follow him.

A few minutes into the new tunnel, the Indian paused. He pointed.

'Be careful to step where I step, or you will fall into this hole.'

He bent and seizing a stone tossed it into the hole. Long moments passed before Hannah heard a distant splash, and knew that at the bottom of this hole, many feet deep, was a pool or an underground river.

Leading John Lucus, and staying close upon the heels of the Indian, they skirted the hole. Hannah shuddered, thinking how horrible it would be to stumble inadvertently into the chasm. She shivered and walked closer to the Indian as he led them around the far side of the hole in the cavern floor. John Lucus courageously stepped where she stepped, clinging stoutly to her hand, uttering no sound.

It seemed to Hannah they walked for miles and for hours. Finally they turned off this tunnel into a room smaller than the one where they had first been held. The Indian paused and turned to them.

'Here you will be safe. I will come and get you when the bad men have left. Do not worry. I will see that you return safely to your home.'

He went to a small pile of leaves and twigs, old and dried from perhaps centuries in the cave, he struck a flint over them and a spark held. A leaf smouldered and burst into a small flame.

The Indian rose. 'There is water.' He pointed to a small pool of water made by moisture seeping from the walls. 'Drink little. Do not think of food. Do not be afraid. I will be back when it is safe for you to leave.' And as suddenly as he had appeared, he was gone.

Hannah glanced around her. There was a pile of broken branches and chunks of wood against the far wall of the cave, enough for several hours, she judged. The water in the pool would be sufficient to sustain them. But, the question would not leave her mind, how long would it be until the Indian came again? There was no way she could find her way out of the cave. She was lost as to directions. She was at the mercy of one who might be a spirit, only part man. Would he come for them?

This she mulled over in her mind, with no answer forthcoming. She pulled her son close to her side and, frightened almost to despair, sat staring into the fire.

TWELVE

Luke stood on the porch of his home. Black Hawk, Red Feather and One Foot sat about on chairs fashioned out of the oak on the ranch. Ben Thompson stood leaning against a porch post, rolling a cigarette.

'We leave at first light in the morning,' Luke told them, his voice grim. 'Pack grub for three days at least, take both rifles and pistols, with at least a hundred shells for each. Canteens, a blanket and tarp. We are going to stay out there until we find them.'

Thompson stirred. The Indians eyed him stoically. 'There were no tracks. How do you know where they went, which way?'

Luke nodded at Black Hawk. 'He knows where their camp was. We'll start there. If no one is there, we'll follow tracks until we find them. They will tell us where Hannah and John Lucus are.

'I don't want no shooting, unless I shoot first. But don't worry about captives. Shoot to kill. After what they have done to Hannah and my son they don't deserve to live.'

It was still dark when they finished breakfast. They had roped out their mounts, with an extra horse for Hannah and the boy. Luke mounted and looked at them, his face grim in the dim light of a dawn just breaking.

'Let's go,' he said. 'Every moment counts.'

'Camp there,' Black Hawk said pointing.

Luke eyed the terrain. 'I've been in this valley ten years or more,' he told Ben Thompson. 'But I've not been in this part.' He nodded to Black Hawk and Red Feather. 'Go see if there are any men about the campsite. I think he must have had most of them with him on the drive.'

The two Indians slid from their ponies and moved quickly and silently away from the others. Luke watched and blinked. They were there, in view, and suddenly gone. He marveled at the Indians' ability to blend into the land, moving silently and easily, becoming as one with the world about them. Centuries of training, he mused. Something a white man would take a lifetime to achieve. He was aware that mountain men, those coming into the wilderness and remaining for a lifetime, were much like the Indian. They had been compelled to be so to be able to live.

Luke and the others slid from their saddles and rested, leaning against the horses, speaking, if at all, in quiet voices that carried to their ears only.

Suddenly Black Hawk, shortly followed by Red Feather, appeared out of the sage and mesquite about them. Black Hawk looked at Luke.

'Not there,' he said. 'Camp empty. All gone away.'

It was fully dark when Josh Carter and Jim Taylor had arrived at the campsite. Milo Swartz was there, broiling a rabbit over a small fire. Josh dismounted and came to the fire. He poured himself a cup of java from the ever-present pot and stood sipping, his eyes on Swartz.

'Did you do what I told you?' he asked.

Swartz nodded shortly. 'They're in the cave like you said.'

Josh looked about him. 'Where's Buck?'

Swartz shrugged. 'He said this rabbit wasn't enough for the two of us. He went out before dark to find one, an' ain't come back yet.' Swartz grinned. 'Maybe a catamount got him.'

Jim Taylor came to the fire, having tended to the horses. He looked at Josh.

'What's your plans now, boss. The woman and boy are in the cave. Where do we go from here?'

Carter laughed. 'With the woman and son in our paws, we can get anything we want from Luke Kane.' He turned to Swartz. 'Go bring Hannah and the boy here.'

Swartz shrugged and going up the slope to the cave, made a torch. He lighted it and entered the cave. In perhaps thirty minutes he was back. He hurried to the fire and faced Carter.

'They ain't there,' he said, his face filled with an inwardly felt guilt.

'Ain't there? Didn't you take them into the cave?'

Swartz nodded, his forehead covered with sudden sweat. 'Yeah. I built them a little fire, and give her a blanket. The blanket is there, an' boss...'

Josh looked at him quizzically. 'Well?'

'Boss, Buck Leonard is layin' in there, dead. Plugged in the shoulder an' gut. An' the woman an' boy are gone.'

Carter paled, his body shook with suppressed anger, mingled with sudden fear.

'Get your gear together,' he ordered. 'We're leaving here right now. We're goin' into Red Rock an' get the boys outta that jail. Then we're comin' back here and take this valley from Kane, burn his house an' barns an' either kill him, or run him outta the country.'

'Boss, what do you think happened to the woman an' kid?' asked Taylor quietly. 'Someone must have found them.'

'I don't know, an' right now, I don't care. They're gone, an' I'll be blamed for their disappearance. We gotta get the boys here in a hurry an' tear this valley apart.'

'You can go back to where the bad men were camped,' he said. Hannah, lost in her thoughts looked up, startled, and saw the old Indian, standing across the chamber from her and Lucus. He had appeared as he had before, suddenly and unheralded by any noise or presence.

'Your husband and his men are there. You will be safe now. Come, follow me and step carefully where I tell you.' John Lucus leaned forward and looked at the dimly outlined figure of the ancient Indian.

'Are you real?' he asked, his voice curious and seemingly unafraid. 'Or are you a ghost like our old cook tells about?'

The lips of the Indian moved in a slight smile. 'I am what you think I am, real or ghost. Your mind will tell you, and you will believe what it tells you, no matter what others say. Come now, I will lead you back to the cave entrance. From there you will be able to return to the camp and will find your man – your father.' The old head nodded to John Lucus and the slight smile came again. 'You will become fine strong man. Let your mind and heart guide you. Look, listen and learn.'

The figure turned and Hannah and John Lucus followed him. The boy seemed un-afraid; Hannah moved cautiously, not really believing what she was seeing and hearing, but willing to trust it. The moving figure was all she had to keep herself and her son alive.

An hour later she stood before the opening

of the cave. She glanced over at the body of Buck Leonard and a wave of guilt swept through her. She had killed a man, taken a human life. She would always regret the fact, yet she knew that had she not been strong enough to protect herself against Leonard, she would never have felt clean again.

She glanced back to speak her appreciation to the ancient Indian, but he was gone.

Taking John Lucus by the hand she led him to the opening of the cave and stepped through. Her man would be there, the old Indian had assured her.

In the darkening of the evening, Luke knelt beside the ashes of the camp-fire and stirred them.

'They haven't been gone long,' he said. 'There are live coals here yet.' He rose and looked about him. 'We'll trail them in the morning, spend the night here. I want to know who they contact in the area. Whoever it is, they are as guilty as Carter and his crew.'

'Luke, look over there coming around that clump of sage.' One Foot nudged Kane with an elbow.

Hannah and John Lucus appeared from back of the large clump of sage and stood looking at the camp. Kane stared at them, unbelieving, and then ran towards them, his face illuminated with surprise and happiness.

She threw herself into his arms and clutched him, her body shaking. Luke felt the clasp of young arms about his legs and reached down, to gather his son into their embrace. Her lips caressed his bearded cheeks and her tears wet his face. John Lucus hugged him and looked up into his face with the childish expression that said I will never let you go away again.

Finally they untangled their arms and Luke led them back to the fire. 'Someone get a fire going. I know they are starved.'

'Give us some water,' Hannah's voice was raspy with dryness. 'All we've had has been a little moisture that drained into a shallow rock cup.' One Foot handed her his canteen, and Hannah passed it first to her son. 'Drink slowly, just a few swallows,' she directed him.

After drinking from the canteen, she sat down on a blanket Luke placed by the fire. Her face was sallow, pale from the time in the dark cave. In a low voice, interspersed by long pauses, she related their experiences since being abducted from the ranch. After a long silence she raised her eyes to Kane's.

'I killed a man, Luke,' she whispered.

He saw the pain in her face and drew her hand into his. 'Who was it, honey?'

She hesitated and then said, 'One of the men who took us from the ranch. You fought him in town one time. Buck Leonard.'

Kane's face grew dark. 'Buck Leonard. If you killed him, he deserved no less. Anyone who would do what he did to you and John Lucus, ain't fit to live among other people.'

He squeezed her hand and put a comforting arm about her shoulders. 'You did what you had to do under the circumstances. You'll regret having had to do it, but don't blame yourself. You did what you had to do.' The others, hearing her, nodded agreement with his words.

Food was prepared, a canteen of water given to both Hannah and John Lucus, and the two ate the first full meal since their abduction. At last they finished and moved back from the fire. Hannah leaned against Kane, who placed his arms about her and held her close to him. How nearly he had come to losing her, he could not fully know.

But her hurt and distress was his to bear with her.

John Lucus looked over at One Foot who stood beyond the fire from them.

'One Foot, there was an Indian in the cave,' he said.

One Foot looked at him without speaking.

'Really,' the boy contended, 'and he called himself "The Old One".'

Kane looked at Hannah. She nodded and then motioned for him to be quiet.

One Foot stirred and came around the fire and knelt on the blanket beside the boy. 'Tell me more,' he said, his face expressionless.

'Well,' the boy collected his thoughts and continued, 'he came all at once. We didn't even hear him, but there he was! He was old, white hair, funny clothes, all made of animal skins, I guess. A strange kind of light seemed to come from him. In the dark of the cave we could see him clearly, and when he spoke, we could understand him.' John Lucus was thoughtful for a moment. 'I think he saved our lives, for he led us to a secret chamber in the cave, and on the way, there was a big, big hole in the floor. He showed us how to get by it without falling.'

The Indian stirred and looked at Hannah.

She nodded her agreement with John Lucus.

'Then he led us back to the front of the cave, and told us you would be here. We came out of the cave and there you were! And, boy, were we glad!'

Sudden emotion moved across the old man's normally stoic face. He took the boy's chin in his hand and gently turned it so he looked deeply into John Lucus's eyes.

'My young friend has been honored,' he said softly. 'No one in my tribe, nor in my memory has ever seen The Old One. But the story is, that the one who does see him will have nothing but good happen in his life. You will know great goodness, my young friend, and live to a very old age. The Old One has willed this for you.'

It was noon when Josh Carter, Swartz and Taylor arrived in Red Rock. They scouted the town and found that the sheriff, Clarence Holland, was away to Cheyenne on business and would not be back until the next week. Bud Fisher, one of the deputies, was left in charge of keeping the peace in Red Rock, and guarding the prisoners until they could be brought to trial.

'Just right,' Josh told the other two with

him. 'The deputy will bunk down in the sheriff's office. We'll bust in an' take care of him. With him out of the way, we'll take the boys back to our camp, an' make our plans. Before he can shake a stick, we'll have Luke Kane where I have wanted him for years.'

THIRTEEN

The three rustlers rolled into their blankets after the saloons closed, hidden in the shadows of the livery stables. They wished it to appear that they had left town. At midnight Josh woke and stirred the others. Quietly they saddled their mounts and led them down the street to the sheriff's office. No one was up and about. One sleepy dog woofed at them from a porch, but did not bark. They hitched their horses to the rail in front of the office, and stepped quietly up on to the boardwalk.

'Swartz, you keep guard at the door,' Josh had directed. 'Taylor and I will take care of what has to be done inside.'

Swartz took his stand beside the door, keeping his eyes on the street. The town was silent, a window here and there glowed with a dim light, as though someone was sleeping with a light on. The door to the office was locked.

'Break it in,' whispered Josh. 'I'll be right behind you and will cold-cock the deputy before he can open his eyes.'

Taylor gathered himself and slammed into the door. The flimsy inside latch gave way and Taylor slid to a stop across the room. Bud Fisher, the deputy, was soundly asleep, and roused himself drowsily, in time to catch Josh's gun barrel across the temple. He fell back on to the bunk, knocked unconscious by Josh's slashing blow to the head.

Josh turned from the inert body of the deputy and stepped to the desk. He jerked open a drawer, and saw the ring of cell keys. He seized them and moved to the nearest cell, where half of his rustler outfit were watching him with wary eyes.

He paused with the keys in his hand. 'Boys, I am goin' to turn you loose, with one condition. You will do one more job for me. After that you are on your own. I'd suggest making dust from this territory, for the law will be on you like a buzzard on day-old dead rabbit.'

'You just let us out, Josh,' one of the men said. 'We'll work with you.' The others nodded their agreement.

'You all make it to the livery and take hosses. We'll meet at the camp where we were when we drove them cattle to the railhead. Once you are all there, I'll tell you what the deal is going to be. If any one of you tries to back out of the deal, after I've got you out of jail, I'll shoot him down where he stands.' He eyed each of them grimly. 'Understand?' There was unanimous agreement once again. Nodding, he unlocked the cell door. Moving to the next cell, where the rest of the men were caged, he looked them over.

'You heard what I said to the rannies in the next cell. I give you the same deal.'

'Just unlock the door, Josh,' one of them said. 'We'll help you an' then high-tail it to other parts.'

In a few minutes they were all out of the cells. Josh handed them their six-guns which hung on nails on one wall of the room. They strapped on the weapons, took hats from a hall-tree beside the door, and were ready to leave.

'Go get your hosses,' Carter told them. 'We'll meet you at the camp. A couple of you break into the mercantile and get a sack of vittles. George Holt usually keeps a bottle or two of good whiskey around. Slip them into the bag, too. Now, get goin' an' be quiet about it.'

In a moment the room was empty except for Carter, Taylor and Swartz, who still stood guard at the door. Carter bent over the deputy and saw that he was breathing. He would be out for several hours and wake with a horrible headache, which would be extended into a greater agony when he had to face the sheriff with empty cells.

Leaving the sheriff's office, now empty of inmates except for Harley Flynn who was sleeping off a drunken spree in the third cell. Harley was a frequent visitor for the same reason, but had yet been unable to con a free meal and a nip of barleycorn out of the sheriff to ease his stomach before leaving.

Josh and his two companions followed the dust of the men just let out of the jail. He was certain that one or two of them would slip away before they arrived at the camp-site. But he was not going to chase them down. He would meet them and square the deal some day down the line. At the moment his mind was completely set upon getting his crew together and making a raid upon Luke Kane and his ranch.

The morning following their return to the ranch, Hannah related her and John Lucus's experience to Luke. He listened grimly, holding her in his arms and hugging her as she sobbed out her picture of Buck Leonard's attempt to assault her. Finally she was stilled and nestled against his chest, her tears dampening his shirt.

'The Old One,' Luke asked, after she had rested several minutes. 'Was this just a figment of John Lucus's vivid imagination, a momentary dream?'

She shook her head slowly. 'No. No dream. I do not know what or who he was. But *something* was there. It spoke English. It looked Indian, dressed as we have seen sketches of elderly chiefs or warriors. He or it did lead us. He led us into a room that he said was only known to his people of long ago. Then he came back and told us you were coming and he led us out to the opening of the cave. A dim figure, outlined in a kind of mist.'

She twisted around and looked him in the eyes. 'Luke, whatever he or it was, your wife and son are here safe because of him.'

He tightened his hug about her. 'If I ever

meet him or it I will give him my thanks for taking care of you both.'

John Lucus seemed unaffected by his experience. He entered into his usual boyhood activities, racing around the ranch on his small, piebald pony, getting in the Indians' way as they worked about the barns and sheds. They loved him and took time to talk with him, and he was often in their lodges, playing with their boys, making small bows and arrows, happy and contented as only a child, loved and cared for, can be.

One morning, following breakfast, he looked at his father for a long moment. Luke noticed his concentration.

'What's the matter, John Lucus? Something on your mind?'

The boy was silent for another long moment and then nodded, slowly. 'Yes, there's something I need to tell you, Dad, but I'm not sure you will believe me.'

'Try me, son. You aren't in the habit of spinning long yarns, so I reckon whatever you have to say will be worth listenin' to.'

John Lucus was silent another long moment and then said softly, 'I saw him again last night, Dad.'

Luke watched his son's face, saw the earnest expression. 'Who did you see?'

'The Old One,' John Lucus said quietly. 'He came to my room and talked to me.'

Luke was silent. How to answer this? He could tell by his expression that the boy wanted to be believed, yet knew his father did not fully accept the fact that an ancient Indian had saved them from harm in the cave.

'Was it a dream, son?'

The boy shook his head. 'No, Dad. Not a dream. Yet not *really* real. He was hard to see and his voice was not loud. But I heard every word. He had a message for me to give to you.'

Luke studied the face of his son. He could see that John Lucus was in earnest about what he had seen and heard. An ancient Indian had saved him and his mother in the cave. Now he appeared to the boy in a dream, or in some strange way. And there was no doubt John Lucus believed what he had ... dreamed? Luke shook his head.

'It is hard to believe, son, but just what was the message?'

His son hesitated a moment. 'Dad, he said that there were bad men gathering to harm us. They will attack us very soon and there will be much blood.'

Luke eyed his son's face carefully. 'Son,

159

that is a mighty bad message. And if it came from some other way, I'd be worried. But – from your dream Indian? I – I just can't believe it is more than a bad dream and it made an impression upon you.' He sighed and shook his head. 'Just a dream, John Lucus. That must be what it was.'

John Lucus fell silent. Finally he got up and wandered away from the house, toward the tack shed where One Foot was working on a lariat. He sat down on a saddle and watched the old Indian's fingers as they plaited the soft leather, crisscrossing it and twisting it into a braid, adding to the length of the lariat.

'Young Kane has a lot on his mind,' said the old Indian. 'What stirs his brain so to make his face this solemn?'

John Lucus then told One Foot what he had related to his father. The old Indian listened carefully as he worked. When the boy was finished and fell silent, One Foot laid aside his work and sat looking at John Lucus. Finally he spoke.

'This is important message the Old One has brought you,' he said seriously. 'Do you believe the Old One speaks true?'

John Lucus hesitated and then nodded. 'Yes,' he said. 'The Old One saved our lives in the cave. Why would he tell me this if it were not true?'

One Foot nodded. 'You are right, John Lucus. White men sometimes speak with forked tongue. Indians do not, and the Old One, could not, for he is sent from the Great Spirit. You have again been honored.' He rose and lifted John Lucus to his feet with a gentle hand. 'Say no more about this to anyone. I will take care of it and when the time comes I will tell your father what must be done.'

John Lucus nodded solemnly and left the shed, the burden the ancient Indian spirit had placed upon his heart lifted.

Within an hour Red Feather was sent on a journey, and Black Hawk was on his way to watch for the rustlers, and to see if they returned to their former campsite at the far end of the valley.

Clarence Holland sat behind his desk in the sheriff's office in Red Rock, and looked at his deputy.

'Did you see any of them that broke in here? Get a look at their faces?'

The deputy rubbed the knot on his head left there by the gun barrel that had been laid across his skull. 'I think I did,' he told the sheriff. 'Just a glimpse before my lights went out.'

'Wa'al, who do you think it was?'

The deputy grimaced. 'I think it was Josh Carter. I kinda recollect a flash of his face as I fell back on the bunk. I don't remember anything after that 'til I woke up with old Harley Flynn shakin' me, an' askin' if I would lend him a dollar for breakfast.'

Clarence sat in deep thought. Josh Carter. He had escaped the roundup of the rustlers at Washakie a few weeks ago. The rustlers were all out of jail, and the judge was not due in for the trial for another week. He considered and decided that Carter and the gang with him were going back to their old hideout at the far end of Paradise Valley, and if that was so...

Luke Kane was in need of help!

FOURTEEN

'Swartz, go in the cave an' see if you can figure out what happened to Hannah Kane an' the boy,' Josh Carter ordered the man who had last seen the two they had

162

kidnapped, who had seemingly disappeared into the depths of the cave.

Carter and his men were back at the former campsite, forming plans to make a run up the valley against Luke Kane. To Carter, the desire to get the best of Kane for once was an overriding passion. That Hannah and her son had suffered and perhaps died because of his hatred of the rancher was of no consequence. As he had once said to Jim Taylor when the latter had backed away from the kidnapping idea, 'you can't make a omelet without breakin' an egg'.

Now, once again in place to bring war against his hated enemy, Carter could not help but wonder what really had happened to Hannah Kane and her son.

'Aw, boss. I don't want to go down in there again. It's dangerous an' it's spooky. Besides, Buck Leonard's remains are there, an' he'll be smellin' by now.'

'That won't kill you,' Carter snapped. 'Go on, see if you can get some idea what happened to the woman an' boy.'

Swartz left grumbling but was back in a short time. 'They ain't in there, boss,' he said.

Carter jerked around and looked at him.

'What do you mean, they ain't there?'

'Their tracks come out of the cave an' I followed them right here to the camp. Someone come an' got 'em.'

Carter glared at him. 'Jim, you've done some trackin',' he said to Taylor. 'See if you can find their tracks around the camp here. An' any others that don't belong to us.'

Taylor left the fire and moved away from the circle. He followed Swartz's path, walking carefully to one side of it. He saw that Swartz was correct. Light footprints in a patch of dust indicated Hannah's smaller foot, and there nearby were the footprints of a child. Moving outward from the circle, wider and wider, he found hoof prints and boot prints that did not belong to any of those in Carter's gang. Finally he reported this to Carter.

'Swartz was right about the woman and boy,' he said. 'Their tracks come right into the camp area. Our movin' about has blotted out some of them, but she was here with the boy. Then, there's been others here. More hoss prints and a couple of men. Someone has got her out of the cave and took her away.' He eyed Carter firmly. 'I'd say it was Kane and one of his Indians, for I saw a moccasin print.'

Carter stared into the fire. Luke Kane was on to him. He might not know Carter had gotten his entire rustler gang out of the jail, but he knew this was their former campsite and he would be watching. Carter knew he must work fast if he was to achieve what he had in mind. Did he have enough men?

He voiced this to Taylor. 'How many are we? Eight, nine?' He eyed the group about the camp circle, counting them. Counting the one watching the hosses, there were nine of them. 'That oughta be enough to take Kane's place. There's only Kane, his wife and kid. An' Swartz said they seen three Injuns around the barns. Injuns can't shoot worth a hoot.'

'Frum what you've told us about the woman, I suspect she can shoot a rifle as good as most men,' Swartz said. 'So, you had better count on her.'

Carter shrugged. 'We don't want to give our plan away. So, Jim, you and one other go into Washakie, an' get us enough vittles for at least a week. We'll kill a beef an' have it ready when you get back.'

In a short time the two men left and Carter gathered the rest of the outlaws about him and began to outline his plan. It was simple enough. Slip up on the ranch house during the night, wait until first light, and attack. No one would be aware of their presence. Even if Kane put out guards and watchers they would not be seen as they moved into place during the night. So, it should be a complete surprise.

'How about the woman an' the kid?' asked one of the men.

Carter shrugged. He had never forgotten the times Hannah had rejected him, both as a youth and as a man. Even when she was married to his cousin, the former sheriff of Red Rock, he had made moves at her. But she had laughed at him. There was no time to play nursemaid now. She had to be put away the same as anyone else. Besides, as Swartz had reminded him, she was another rifle against them.

'She's takin' her chances, just like the others. If she gets in your way, shoot her.'

'An' the boy?'

Carter glared at the man. 'Nits grow up into lice,' he said. 'I want every member of that family down. An' watch out for them Injuns. They'll be fightin' their style. Keep your eyes peeled for them.'

The men stared at him. In the minds of several was the knowledge that in the west womenfolk were treated with respect. And

166

children were never expected to be treated as enemy. Just ignore them and let others see to their welfare. But they listened to their boss, and no one voiced an opinion.

'Get your rest now,' he ordered. 'Stay close to the camp, in case someone might be wandering this way. When Taylor and Slim return we'll eat good, an' three nights from now give Luke Kane a lesson he, nor no one else, expects.'

Kane stood on the shelf before the entrance to the valley. Not far from him two of the women, belonging to Red Feather and Black Hawk, worked about the lodges, one hoeing in the patch of corn near the lodge, and the other laying out some damp clothes on rocks to dry, having pounded and washed them in the creek.

Where were the two Indian men? He had not seen either of them for a day, at least. He did not question One Foot about them, for Black Hawk was the hunter of the family and spent much time in the forest foothills of the valley. It was not unusual for Hannah to walk out upon the back porch of a morning and find the haunch of a recently slaughtered buck, wrapped in part of the skin. Black Hawk shared his game with the white people – after all Kane had allowed them to find shelter and make a home in the valley.

Kane looked out over the valley. It spoke of peace. The sun was warm, but not hot. A light breeze touched him, coming down from the mountain slopes. Below in a meadow he saw the few cattle grazing, those missed by Carter and his men when they made their sweep of the pastures and collected his beef and horses.

Such a beautiful place, he mused. Ten years we have been here and built our home and our ranch. Food in plenty, with exception of certain staple items which they bought in George Holt's mercantile every so often. But he and his wife and son were content here, and needed no emotional contact with the outside world. He sighed. But the Good Book told them, as Hannah had read to him, that one time there was turmoil in heaven, and a dark angel had been banished. If there was trouble in Paradise, he mused, then why not expect it to visit them in their own little paradise? He shook his head.

Carter. Josh Carter. What drove the man? True, Kane had thrashed him once years ago, and at another time had knocked him unconscious and left him tied with his own kerchief and belt. Can hatred of a happening, of a person, last that long? His face tightened as he thought of Carter. According to One Foot, he had somehow gathered his gang together again. How did they get out of jail? Had his friend Clarence Holland, the sheriff, been killed in their escape? And if this had happened, then One Foot was undoubtedly correct in that Carter and his gang of outlaws were once again in the valley. Were they bold enough to return to the same campsite, knowing that Luke would have located it by now, and had been there and rescued his wife and son from the cave?

He sighed. There was only one thing to do. He, with One Foot and the old Indian's nephews, Red Feather and Black Hawk, should be able to hold them off. He had plenty of guns and ammunition, and there was a cistern at the back of the house, with enough water to last indefinitely. And there was plenty of food. But if Carter had gotten his entire gang together, then it would be five of them against nine or ten, perhaps more, should Carter have recruited others to join them.

One Foot had accepted John Lucus's story

of his vision and the message of the Old One. Luke shook his head. It had to be a dream, a figment of a boy's imagination. Indian lore of the West was filled with such stories. Young men, to gain their manhood, went into the wilderness alone and stayed several days fasting, until they received a vision, out of which would come their adult name. Black Bear saw and wrestled with such an animal in his vision during his fasting. Strong Eagle had the vision of being guarded by an eagle, who advised him of life ahead. These stories were replete with strange visions. Simply because he was a white boy did not mean he could not have such a vision or dream, having heard these stories all his young life.

But Luke Kane could not accept such things. Even when his wife, Hannah, swore they were led to safety in the cave by such an apparition, an ancient Indian wrapped in some kind of misty light – even then he could not believe it.

He stood in the early morning light looking out over the valley, his life, his home. The shadow of an eagle crossed his face and its calls reached to him. Was it warning him? He shook his head and left the shelf, his mind caught up with what was necessary to prepare for him and his family's safety, should the Old One and the vision of his son be true.

Carter, along with Jim Taylor, had indeed recruited four more men to join them in taking Luke Kane's valley away from him. He and Taylor had gone into the saloon at Washakie the day following the release of the prisoners.

'I'll see that you are paid well for helping me out, and you can come on back here, or go wherever you want to go. I'd suggest leaving the territory. But you will leave with money in your pockets.'

'Is this the Luke Kane that was a Texas Ranger a few years back?' one of them questioned him.

Carter nodded. 'But he ain't the fast gun he used to be and he's a settled married man with a kid. So he won't be the hell-raiser he was back then. Got soft in his old age and good life.'

One of the men was tall, slim, mean-eyed and carried two six-guns tied down, shootist style.

'Ah reckon he won't be too hard to deal with,' he drawled. 'I'll go along with you if you let me have first crack at him.'

Carter nodded. 'You're on. He's yours when the time comes.' To himself he thought, 'You'd better be good with them sixes, or Luke Kane will eat you alive and spit you out before breakfast.' Mentally he was pleased to recruit another who would follow his orders with only the object of good money when the job was done.

He and Taylor left Washakie with four who knew their way along the owl-hoot trails and whose faces appeared on posters in lawmen's offices all over the territory. He now had thirteen men and himself. Luke Kane's valley was as good as his for the taking!

FIFTEEN

Clarence Holland, with one of his deputies, rode into Paradise Valley through the secret crevice and was passed on by One Foot, who was guarding the portals. Luke Kane, coming out of a shed near the barn saw them coming off the shelf, leading down to the corrals. He stood, waiting for them, as they pulled up and stepped from the saddle.

'Howdy, Luke,' Clarence greeted him. He nodded at the deputy. 'I guess you remember Bud Fisher from our trip into Washakie after your beef an' hosses.'

Kane smiled and shook hands with both. 'What brings you to this place at this time, Clarence? Someone around here broke the law?'

The sheriff's face was solemn. He shook his head. 'Nope. But Josh Carter broke his rustler gang out of jail. I figure they come back up there,' he nodded toward the mountains at the end of the valley, 'an' probably are makin' ready to raid you again.'

Luke grimaced. 'Come on down to the house, boys, and have cup of coffee. Vittles if you feel the need. We'll talk there.'

Around the long table in the mess hall, with cookie pouring coffee and placing a plate of 'bear sign' before them, Luke looked at the two lawmen.

'I think you are probably right as to where Carter has holed up at. But, I don't have enough men to go and dig them out. There are hundreds of places they could hole up and then run from and we'd spend our time getting little accomplished.'

'What do you intend doin'?' asked the sheriff.

Kane shrugged 'If you and the deputy want to take a hand in my troubles, you might stick around for awhile. I suspect Carter is not going to wait for us to come to him. I think he'll be here in a day or two. With you we'd have seven men. And Hannah and the boy will be safe in this house. The walls are foot-thick oak and the roof is shale.'

The sheriff nodded. 'We'll stay. Bud, why don't you go put our hosses in the corral an' look about the place for some good spots for a rifleman.'

Bud nodded. 'Thems the best "bear signs" I ever et,' he complimented cookie on the doughnuts, thanked him for the coffee, and left to see to the horses.

During the day Luke and the sheriff decided on places where the seven men might make their stand, when Carter and his men sprung their attack. Luke was working in the tack shed in the early evening when he heard a step behind him and he whirled round, his hand slapping his six-gun butt. One Foot stood in the doorway.

'One Foot, you nearly scared the daylights out of me. What's up?'

One Foot stepped aside and four Indians

crowded the doorway. They looked at Luke stoically. He noticed that while one or two of them carried rifles, at least a couple were carrying the short, stubby war bow used only in fighting their enemies, or in hunting the buffalo.

'Who are these men? And what are they doing here?' asked Kane.

'These men are of my village. I tell them about Carter and how he come into your valley and do bad things. They want to help you.'

Kane looked at the solemn faces. The men were dressed mostly in whiteman clothes, with added belts and straps of leather, undoubtedly made by their women from animal hides. Two were rather tall for Indians of this area, two were of medium height. All appeared strong and watched his face with sharp eyes.

Luke nodded. 'You are welcome and we can use all the help we can get. One Foot will place you where you can do the most good. The wives will feed you in their lodges. I am glad you are here. We need all the help we can get. Thank your chief for letting you come.'

One Foot looked at one of the taller men. 'He is Strong Arrow, chief of our tribe. He speaks your tongue and understands what you say.'

The tall Indian, indicated by One Foot pointing his chin, looked at Luke.

'I am Strong Arrow. We are glad to help our white brother, and the friend of One Foot and his family.'

One Foot gestured and the Indians stepped away from the doorway. He looked at Luke.

'We be close by. When Black Hawk comes with report, I will tell you.'

Luke suddenly felt better. He did not want a battle; however, if it was inevitable, he was glad to have more men. With himself, Thompson, the sheriff and a deputy, along with seven Indians, there were now eleven to fight off the invaders. He sighed and shook his head. He thought, I should have killed Josh Carter ten years ago, and we wouldn't he in this bind.

Luke, Thompson and the sheriff were sitting on the front porch. It was nearing bedtime. Guards were out and in place. Luke and the others with him would share four-hour shifts. They smoked and talked quietly. Thompson had remained simply because he had a score to settle with Jim Taylor. The sheriff was interested in recapturing those he could of the rustlers and holding them for trial. Kane simply wanted to save his house and barns from fire, for he did not doubt that Carter would resort to setting the buildings ablaze if the opportunity were before him. He was an evil man, with evil thoughts, and twisted values of right and wrong. Anything was possible, Kane realized, and he was determined to fight savagely for what was his.

Two dark shadows slipped up on to the porch: One Foot with Black Hawk at his side.

'They come,' the Indian scout reported.

'Where are they now?' Kane asked him.

Black Hawk pointed. 'Not far. Behind hill. Will come when night has paled,' he said, referring to dawn.

The Indians disappeared from the porch, to take their places in the guarding and protection of the ranch. Ben Thompson and the other men sought their blankets for what sleep they might be able to get.

Luke Kane stood on the porch looking out over his ranch. Hannah came and stood beside him, putting an arm about his waist, leaning against him.

'Come to bed, honey,' she urged. 'Get

177

whatever rest you can.'

He looked out over the land, his arm about his wife protectively. Inside was their son, who would one day own all this. He would fight to save the future for his son. He looked out towards the hill behind which Black Hawk said the enemy was waiting.

They were there, waiting for light to move.

They were coming.

SIXTEEN

Josh Carter paced most of the night. He and his outlaws had arrived at the spot decided on earlier after being scouted by Swartz, who had traveled the area when he kidnapped Hannah and John Lucus. It was on the slope of a hill, out of sight of the ranch buildings, but close enough to move up quietly when it became light enough to attack.

His mind was filled with many things. How successful would his attack be? Should he burn the barns and the house? Most of all, he gritted his teeth at the thought, he wanted to see Luke Kane fall, with a bullet through his heart. He finally sought his blankets, to lie there casting about what might happen in the future should he fail. But he could not fail! This would be his last chance to get Kane, for if he failed, he would be chased throughout the West. Only a short time before he knew he must arouse out those who would bear the brunt of the attack, he fell into a fitful sleep.

Jim Taylor had a similar night, thinking and wondering just what he had gotten himself into. He had come into the area merely to escape the law further south. All he had sought was a job on a ranch, a chance to disappear quietly into the range and among cattle. But it did not ride that way, and now he was embroiled in a feud, of which he knew little of the cause. When this was over, he decided, he would ride out and find other pastures – perhaps even more secluded.

Carter woke as the sky began to pale. He rose and stretched. He rubbed his face and scratched his scalp and put on his sombrero. Going to each man, he kicked a foot, boot-encased or not.

'Get out of them blankets of comfort,' he yelled. 'Time's awastin'. Up an' at 'em!'

There were curses and grumbles, but the men rose and rolled their blankets.

'No breakfast?' grumbled one.

'No. Take a good drink from your canteen, and chew on a piece of jerky. No fires. We ride.' He glanced at the eastern sky, where pink was just beginning to spread across the mountain tips. 'A quick quirly as you saddle up. Get a move on!'

Watching from a mesquite bush just across the peak of the slope, Black Hawk saw the activity and left his place of hiding, racing down the slope of the hill away from the outlaws. Kane was up and standing on the porch, smoking, when the Indian came up.

'They get ready to ride,' Black Hawk reported.

Kane tossed his cigarette to the ground and stepping off the porch, ground it into the dirt with a boot heel.

'Get the others out and into their places,' he said quietly. 'Give yourself a good place and make every shot count.'

Black Hawk jerked his head, turned and melted into the shadows of the nearest oak, where he knew One Foot was waiting.

Kane aroused those in the house with him. 'Ben and I will take the porch, the front of the house,' he said, when they had gathered in the kitchen where Hannah had a plate of doughnuts and a pot of hot, black coffee waiting for them. She had been up even before Luke, and had thoughtfully prepared something for them. It might be many hours before they could sit down to a meal.

'Clarence, you and your deputy cover the back. Be careful. They will rush us, I know. And they won't attack just one side of the house. Black Hawk said there were eleven of them. So they can't have too many attacking one location. But I'm pretty sure they will all hit us at once.'

The men nodded assent and left the room, to take up their positions for the attack.

'Mount up,' Carter ordered, and the men swung into their saddles. 'Slim,' Carter spoke to one man. 'You hold the hosses in that swale there just below the house. An' Jake,' he nodded to another. 'You high-tail it to the corrals. When we fire the first shot, you open the gates and run the hosses out. Then come up to the barns an' keep watch for them Injuns.' He turned his horse and gigged it with spurs. 'Let's go!' he yelled and the entire group raced to the peak of the slope and toward the large house under the trees.

'Here they come! Keep alert!' Kane saw the first horse and rider burst over the peak of the hill and race, with others directly behind him, straight toward the house. 'Hold your fire until they get close. Make every shot count!'

Grim-faced he watched Josh Carter lead his gang of outlaws toward the house. Fifty yards away they pulled up and dismounted. One man grabbed the reins of the horses and led them to the dip in the land that Carter had indicated. Kane nodded gravely. We are in for a long siege, he thought. They've left their horses and mean to attack on foot, creeping and hiding behind whatever gives them cover. He said as much to the sheriff and Thompson and they both nodded soberly.

Crouched behind the bole of a tree, Carter saw that there were three men barricaded on the front porch.

'Jim, you take two men around to the back. Swartz and I will keep them busy here in front.' With those orders, he leveled his rifle and seeing the bulk of one of the defenders rise briefly from behind a bale of hay, he fired quickly. Ejecting the spent shell he fired again at once and Swartz and the men with him poured lead towards the house.

One thing very soon went wrong for Carter. The man designated to open the corrals raced up to the gate. He was unable to manipulate the heavy poles from horseback, so he dismounted and reached to release the leather thong holding the gate closed.

As he reached there was a soft *whang* and a hiss of something traveling swiftly through the air. He felt a thump in his back and an excruciating pain raced through him. He gasped, and looking down, saw the head of an arrow protruding from his chest. Unable to yell because of a throat full of blood, he seized the arrow shaft at his chest, and attempted to jerk it from his body. He stiffened and quivered and fell, life leaving him in the dust of the corral.

Carter glanced back briefly at the corral and barns and wondered why the animals were still milling around in the enclosure. A bullet slapping the tree trunk beside his head brought his attention back to the moment. He lost his thought and gave several more shots toward the house. Then he clicked on empty. He crouched behind the tree-bole and quickly reloaded the rifle. He heard shots being fired at the back of the house, and others returning fire. Kane had men all over he place, he thought.

One of the men with Taylor, attacking the

back of the house, grew bold. They had traded shots with those guarding the back of the house, with no effect.

'This ain't gettin' us anywhere,' he growled to Taylor. 'I'm gonna slide around the corner there and get close to that window. I'll get the first one that moves.'

'Stay where you are,' Taylor ordered, but the man simply stared at him, and then creeping beyond the barrier of the log where he had hidden, he started toward the house in a crouch.

Clarence Holland, the sheriff, glanced out of the window and saw the man leave his place of concealment and start in a fast crouch toward the back porch. Seeing the direction he was going, the sheriff slipped over to the porch door. A small window beside the door gave him a better view of the back. The man was nearly up to the porch.

The sheriff jerked open the back door and as the Carter man straightened to step up on to the porch, he saw the grim-faced sheriff, holding a leveled rifle.

'Drop your gun an' get in here. Yore goin' back to the hoosegow—'

'Not me, I ain't!' the man yelled and leveled his sixgun for a quick snapshot at the lawman. He hurried his shot and missed.

Clarence squeezed the trigger of his rifle and the slug took the outlaw in the belly, tearing through his body and lodging against his spine. The man screamed and fell, blood spreading about him. Holland closed the door and returned to his place of observation. That's one the county won't have to feed, he thought, and gave his attention to the back areas of the house and the wide lawn.

Carter again glanced at the corrals and saw the horses still inside. He narrowed his gaze and saw Jake, sent to release the horses, lying inert against the gate. A cold feeling swept up his back. Suddenly apprehensive, he turned his attention back to the house. One of the men on the porch apparently caught a glimpse of his movements, and several rounds struck the bole of the tree behind which he crouched.

Three of the outlaw gang had spread out and taken cover behind the tack shed, the equipment building and the barn. They lost sight of each other. The rustler at the tack shed heard a sound back of him and turned to see a tall Indian standing ten feet away, eyeing him silently with dark, gleaming eyes. He whirled around, attempting to bring his rifle to bear on the Indian.

He was too late. The Indian lunged at him, grappled briefly with him and bore him to the ground. The white man glared upward and saw the gleam of a knife blade descending; an instant later he stiffened and jerked, as the blade pierced his heart. Savagely the Indian withdrew the knife, and with a swift motion slit the throat of the white man. He rose to his feet, wiped his blade on the pants of his victim and disappeared beyond the tack shed.

A second outlaw, charged with attacking from the barn, rose up from behind a horse trough and as he did so an arrow swished by him. It narrowly missed him and buried itself into the body of the trough. He whirled around and saw an Indian leaping toward him. He rolled away from his concealment and in finding his feet, raced headlong toward where he thought Carter was hiding. Seeing his boss behind the bole of a huge oak tree, he crawled hurriedly toward him, panting with exertion and fear. He slapped Carter's leg, bringing him swinging around, wide-eyed and throwing down on his with a rifle. The man held up his hands and rolled back from Carter.

'It's me, boss, Hank! Boss, there's Injuns all around us. I just got away from one, an' as I ran past the tack shed I saw one of our men with his throat cut! I'm gettin' out of here! I didn't sign on to fight the whole Injun nation!'

Carter stared at him. 'There was only three Injuns, accordin' to Taylor. He an' Swartz seen them around when they scouted the place. What do you mean, a lot of them?'

'Josh, I saw what one had done to that feller with a cut throat. I got a glimpse of Jake down at the corrals, an' he's got a arrow through his chest. An' one chased me out of the barn just now. You stay if you want, but I'm outta here, right now.'

Carter stared at him, unbelieving. If what the man was saying, then Kane had brought in Indians to fight against him; and Ben Thompson was also said to be in with Kane. But who else could there be in the house? The front and back were both well covered.

He nodded. 'I can't make you stay. But before you go, work your way around back of the house an' see what's goin' on there, see what Taylor thinks of things.'

The man hesitated and then nodded. He crawled away, then, taking a chance he rose and ran across one corner of the yard.

Kane saw a movement among the trees,

and, watching carefully, saw the man leave his concealment and run across the narrow strip of yard. He lined up on the figure as it moved quickly across the dawn-shadowed space, and leading him slightly, he fired. The figure yelled in pain, grabbed a leg and fell, then started crawling toward the trees again. Beside Kane Ben Thompson's rifle spoke. The man stiffened and fell. He scrabbled with his hands a moment or two and then quivered and was still.

Kane shook his head and sighed. 'I hate to see that. But he bought into the fight with Carter, and took his chances.'

Thompson nodded soberly. 'It's too bad to have to take a man's life, even in defense of oneself. But, Luke, that bullet was his today, or next month, when he's on the owl-hoot trails again.'

Luke nodded. 'True, Ben. But that don't make it any easier. I hate to see it or be put into the position where I have to kill or be killed.'

Carter saw it all. He counted. Jake down at the corral, this man, another at the barn. And maybe others. He was fast losing the upper hand in this fight, if he had had it in the first place, which he was beginning to doubt. If the group of hardcases he had assembled were unable to overcome Kane and his defenders, then, what with losses already occurred, he began to deem it unlikely that they would be able to get the job done. He fumed silently. Over a dozen men and they were unable to overcome six or seven. What was it going to take? Fire? Fire? Why not. Set a couple of the sheds afire which would, at least, draw Kane himself from the house.

Carter left his place of concealment and crawled over to where Swartz lay behind a fallen log. He called softly to the outlaw. Swartz turned slightly and saw him crawling across the open space between their hiding places. Two quickly spaced shots brought whistling lead over their area, and Swartz ducked, crouching more deeply into his place of safety. Carter crawled up beside him.

'What's wrong? You hurt?' asked Swartz, his eyes never leaving the porch. The three men there were making it hot for him and Carter.

'I'm OK. But I want to talk to you.'

Swartz grunted. 'Keep your head down. You'll draw their fire, an' they get close enough as it is.'

'That's what I wanted to talk about,'

Carter said. 'We've lost four or five men. We've got to do something to draw Kane out of the house. I want you to get over to the barn and with the men there, set fire to it. Some of the sheds, too.'

Swartz leered at him. 'Afeered of goin' yourself?' he smirked.

Carter scowled. 'I ain't afraid. But someone has to keep this part of the place covered. An' you're better at this Injun kind of fightin' than me. Go on over there, an' get some smoke goin'. That'll bring Kane out.'

Swartz eyed Josh suspiciously. He had figured Carter as cowardly. Now he knew it. But he agreed that the idea of firing the barn and sheds was good. If anything would bring the owner of the spread out of his hiding-place, this would do it.

'All right,' he agreed. 'You get some lead goin' at them fellers on the porch, to keep their attention.' He checked the loads in his rifle and scooted along the ground; keeping low for several yards, he went to do as Carter had ordered.

Swartz was no fool. He was convinced that it was futile to try to get Kane and his defenders out of the house. Perhaps firing the barns and sheds would do the trick. Carter had not informed him of the Indians already reported to be about the barns. When he managed to make his way through a copse of trees and into the barn lot, he was startled to see one of their men sprawled in death before the tack shed. Going closer, he realized this was a death caused by no white man. And in the dust beside the body was the imprint of a moccasin. Indian?

He straightened quickly and glanced about, just as Red Feather slipped around the side of the shed. He ducked and fired quickly. His shot missed and Red Feather leaped back of the shed. Swartz dived behind a horse trough, crawled its length, then sprang to his feet and ran toward the copse of trees he had used as cover on his way to the barns. The Indian leaped into the open again and started after him. Swartz dove for cover behind a small pine, turned, leveled his rifle and fired at the Indian. Red Feather faded into the ground and Swartz left his cover and ran towards the swale where the horses were being held.

He raced down the slope and the horse-holder, seeing him, surmised he was after a horse and pulled a mount about for him.

'What's goin' on?' he questioned Swartz, as the burly man came hurtling down the slope and seized the reins of the horse.

'We're losin' men right and left,' Swartz panted. 'The rest will be along directly. I'm takin' my horse an' one for Carter. We'll be right back.'

He mounted, grabbed the reins of the other mount and spurred up the slope and over the crest of the small hill.

'Carter!' he bellowed.

Carter, hearing the yell, turned and saw Swartz coming. He decided instantly that Swartz had the right idea. Get out of this firefight. Run to fight another day! He raced toward Swartz and as the mount swung about, he leaped into the saddle.

'Taylor!' he yelled, and then spurred the horse away from the trees and up the slope beyond which the horse-handler waited.

Taylor heard the yell. He realized what it meant. Emptying his rifle at the back of the house, spraying the windows and doors, he slipped away from his hiding place and ran toward the draw where the horses were being held. As he arrived he saw Swartz and Carter racing away from the ranch, leaving a roll of dust behind them. He seized a horse, from the handler, then he paused.

'It's over, man, Get on your hoss an' get outta here. Go back to the campsite. We'll see what's next when we all get together.'

With that, he was gone, the horsehandler followed right behind him, leaving the rest of the horses to themselves.

It was quiet around the ranch house. Kane and Thompson roamed the porch and received no fire. Kane saw the roll of dust from the hoofs of the retreating outlaws, and realized the siege was finished. He sighed with relief.

Grimly he thought of the next move. Carter had to be stopped. He mentioned the fact to Thompson, who nodded.

'Let's clean up here. Then follow them. The gang has to be wiped out.'

Kane eyed the disappearing dust of the outlaws. He nodded slowly, his green eyes shooting sparks.

'Let's go get 'em,' he said.

SEVENTEEN

Three grim-faced men left the Kane ranch three days after the siege by Josh Carter and his band of outlaws; Luke Kane, Ben Thompson and the sheriff, Clarence Holland.

They had remained long enough after the attack to round up those escaping when the fighting was over. Five of the attackers were dead. Four were rounded up and held by Holland's deputy to be herded into Red Rock and to jail. The rest escaped, either following Carter and those with him, or scattering to the winds, evading any arrest by the sheriff.

Once things had been taken care of at the ranch, Kane called One Foot to him.

'We are going after Carter. Take care of the place while we are gone. If all goes right we won't be bothered by Josh Carter and his band of rustlers again.'

One Foot nodded stoically. 'Me take care. Other of my tribe will stay until you get back.'

Now, with Black Hawk leading them on the trail of the three outlaws, Kane and those with him were all aware that the final confrontation would be bitter. Death would occur from gunplay in the near future.

The sheriff watched Black Hawk. The Indian followed tracks through sand, rocky terrain and grass-covered expanses.

'I think that he could track a lizard across a hot rock,' the sheriff said, observing the tracker. They had arrived at the former campsite of the outlaws, and were now being led out of the valley through a maze of canyons and streams of cold, mountain water.

Kane nodded. He was silent, thinking ahead. They had been a day and night on the trail now and he had finally realized the possibility of where Josh Carter might be leading his companions. Black Hawk had told them that they were following three riders.

Washakie Post lay in the direction they were heading, Kane surmised. He mentioned this to Black Hawk. The Indian was silent and then nodded.

'Bad men go to Washakie,' he said, his face expressionless. 'They be one day ahead.'

Kane called a halt to rest the horses and to make a cold meal.

'Biscuits and jerkie,' he told his companions. 'Then we head straight for Washakie. It's a railhead for cattle shipment and these three are probably going to stop a train, put their hosses in a car and go. I want to catch them in the town and bring this affair to a conclusion.' The others agreed.

'We'll rest here and then get on the way,' said Kane. 'We'll ride all night and be there before daylight. We just might surprise them.'

Kane was right in thinking Washakie was Carter's destination. He was also correct when he believed they would take a train out of town and out of the territory. Carter gritted his teeth at realizing he had not completed his mission of annihilating Luke Kane and seizing his ranch as his own. Now he was on the run again, and his enemy remained. But there will be another day, he thought grimly. And I'll get Luke Kane into my sights for a reckoning.

Swartz and Taylor were as anxious as Carter to shake the dust of this area from their boots. They not only had Luke Kane after them, but the sheriff for breaking out of his jail. Taylor added another bit of news for them.

'I saw Ben Thompson. He's a killer and boys, he's after me. Been houndin' me ever since I downed a friend of his two years ago.'

'We'll stay here tonight. Tomorrow we will jump the train out of here,' Carter told them. 'I'll find Luke Kane some other time. Now, let's get us some grub an' then hit the blankets. I'm bushed.'

Luke, Holland and Thompson came into

Washakie after midnight. They found the livery and after caring for their horses, bedded down in the loft on blankets and straw.

'We'll be up at daylight. We'll see if Carter and those with him are holed up somewhere near,' said Luke.

Black Hawk had come with them. On hearing Kane's words he slipped away in the darkness. Silently he scouted the town and it was not long before he found Carter's hiding-place in a room above the saloon; their horses being stabled in a shed behind it. Satisfied, he left the center of the town and slipped back to the livery. He lay on a blanket in the shadow of the eaves, keeping watch.

The liveryman came to the stables about dawn and walked in the door to find Kane facing him. Two other men came down the ladder from the loft; three hard-faced men stood looking at him.

'Where is Josh Carter and his men? I know they are here. Where are they staying?' Luke asked him.

The man gulped and shook his head. Black Hawk spoke from the shadows behind them.

'Carter an' men in room above saloon,' he

said. The livery man looked at the expressionless face of the Indian and shivered.

'I never figured on no Injuns. Yeah, Carter an' his men are in a room over the saloon.'

Luke's green eyes glinted. 'You go tell them that we're here. We'll be waiting here for them.'

The man gulped and nodded vigorously and left at a fast walk that turned into a run before he was out of their sight. Luke turned to Black Hawk.

'Did you find their hosses?' Black Hawk nodded.

'Go back now and see if you can lead the hosses out of the shed and turn them loose.' Black Hawk nodded and disappeared into the growing light of the morning.

The liveryman was back less than an hour later, panting from his run. He stumbled into the stable and found Kane standing, waiting for him.

'Well? What did they say?'

The man swallowed, a large Adam's apple sliding up and down his throat.

'Carter ... he said they'd be out in the street afore the saloon at sundown.'

Luke nodded. 'All right. You go on about your business. We'll be around but pay us no mind.' He gestured to Thompson and the sheriff.

'He's cagey, all right. See what he's doing? Sundown, we come down from the stable on Main Street toward the saloon, and the late sun will be right in our eyes. It gives them an advantage, for we'll have to squint out from under our hat-brims to see them.'

'There's one thing we can do, Luke,' said Holland.

'What's that?'

'Go up to their room right now and roust them out. They won't expect us.'

Luke was thoughtful. 'Maybe. But other folks might be hurt with the shooting there is bound to be.'

Black Hawk was standing a few feet away, listening, his face stoic. Luke turned to him.

'Was there anyone with Carter, other than Taylor and Swartz?'

The Indian shook his head. 'No see anyone else.'

Luke moved to the door of the livery and rolled a cigarette. Drawing a deep breath of the smoke, he let it out slowly. He nodded after several minutes. At last he finished his smoke, ground out the butt in the dirt of the livery entrance, and looked at his companions.

'All right. We'll cut the cards our way. Here's what we'll do.'

The sun shone from a cloudless sky, lowering to the mountain rims, its red rays glancing down the main street of the town. The word had gotten out. There was to be a shoot-out in the street come sundown. Bystanders were clustered in doorways, or around windows inside the buildings. Riders coming in and hearing what was going to happen moved their horses off the main street out of danger of stray bullets.

In the saloon Carter finished his beer and looked at Taylor and Swartz who were at the table with him. He picked up his hat from the floor beside his chair and tugged it down over his forehead. The barkeep watched him and knew the fracas was about to begin. Carter stood and stretched.

'It's time, boys,' he said. 'Let's get this over with once and for all.' Taylor and Swartz slid back their chairs and stood, loosening their pistols in their holsters.

The three moved through the room toward the batwing doors. There were several men in the room and a couple of 'soiled doves' kept about the saloon for the entertainment of the customers. They stood close together at the foot of the stairs that led up to rooms where they took their customers for more serious entertainment.

Carter stepped out upon the veranda in front of the saloon entrance. Swartz and Taylor stepped out behind him and spread out, one on either side of him. Carter nodded shortly and stepped out into the center of the street, facing the livery. He noticed with satisfaction that the sun was glinting down, low and red, into the open entrance of the stables. He glanced about him, waiting to see Luke Kane and his friends step out into the sunlight.

'We're here, Josh,' Luke's low voice came laconically from back of them.

Carter paled and whirled, startled. Kane had outguessed him again and now he and Taylor and Swartz faced the glaring, setting sun that obstructed their vision, placing them at the disadvantage he had planned for Kane.

'Carter,' Clarence Holland said sternly, 'unbuckle your gunbelts an' step back. I'm arresting you for rustling cattle and hosses, an' for attackin' the Kane ranch, putting all there in danger of pain or death, including his wife and boy.'

Carter stiffened and crouched, his right

hand trembling above his gun-butt. He shook his head.

'No way,' he yelled, his tones strangling in his rage and sudden apprehension. 'We ain't goin' to no jail.' He looked with glaring hatred at Kane. 'Luke Kane ... I'm callin' you! Draw!'

Carter's hand dropped to his gun-butt and swiftly lifted the weapon from the leather, aiming as the steel left the leather.

He's good, the thought ran through Kane's mind, very good. Somewhere along these lost years, Josh Carter had become a man, a gunman. A prison escapee, leader of a band of cut-throats, rustler and outlaw, Josh Carter had now become a shootist.

Carter's six-gun roared and the slug, meant for his forehead, whistled past Kane's face. Kane turned sideways and quickly drew and leveled his own gun. Carter fired again and Kane lurched back, hit high in the chest. He fired.

Carter was drawing down for his third time when Kane's bullet struck him in the groin. He staggered and attempted to lift his pistol, but Kane's second bullet entered his neck, tearing the great arteries there, and sending Carter to the ground, twisting and clutching his throat.

Ben Thompson drew and fired, his slug taking Jim Taylor in the chest, driving into his heart. Taylor yelled and stiffened and fell, his six-gun falling from his hand. Holland drew and fired as Swartz leveled his pistol at him. The sheriff's bullet struck Swartz's gunhand and tore the weapon from his grasp. He backed away, pale with pain, and raised his hands.

'I'm out of it, stop shootin'.' He lurched to one side and sat down heavily on the edge of the boardwalk.

It all happened in a few minutes. Of six men standing at the beginning of the shoot-out, Kane was on his feet and staggering to lean against the saloon, wounded deeply in the chest. He sighed and slid down the side of the building. Neither Thompson or Holland were injured. Carter and Taylor lay sprawled, dead in the street.

The silence, after the roar of the guns, was deep, disturbed only by the chirping of a bird in a tree across the street from the saloon.

'Gawd,' murmured one of the watching saloon-women, eyeing the wounded men and those dead in the dust of the street, 'sometimes life don't mean much, does it?'

EIGHTEEN

Luke Kane was badly wounded. The bullet had entered high in his chest on the left side and, penetrating his body, it had just missed vital organs and arteries, lodging beneath the skin in the back.

He was carried into an upstairs room of the saloon, and there Ben Thompson and Clarence Holland cared for him. Thompson, wise in the way of gunplay, removed the bullet from his back, cleaned the wound as best he could of cloth fragments, and dressed it with whiskey and horse liniment. The rest was up to constant immediate care, and the ability of a healthy body to mend itself.

After a week he and the sheriff decided Kane was able to withstand a trip to the Lazy L ranch. They hired a buckboard, filled it with a mattress and blankets and with Holland driving and Thompson riding behind the wagon, keeping an eye on the patient, they left Washakie. The sheriff had deputized two men to take Swartz to Red

Rock and put him behind bars, to await whatever the law would decide for him. Black Hawk was sent on ahead to inform Hannah that Luke was being taken to the ranch. One of the Indians would take her there to meet him.

At the ranch Luke was made as comfortable as possible in one of the spacious bedrooms of the ranch house, nursed by the Mexican housekeeper of Rube Lincoln, the ranch owner, and Luke's long time friend. Hannah was there to meet him when he arrived, barely conscious because of the long ride in the buckboard.

Slowly he mended. Doc Somers was brought out from Red Rock and spent three days caring for the wound and watching for any lowering life-signs. But the strong body of Luke Kane would not surrender to the onslaughts of fever, and once the fever was over he was out of danger.

A month after the fight at Washakie, he and Hannah, with John Lucus riding on his pony beside them, left the ranch and climbed the blue mesa. They traveled through the steep-sided crevice and came out upon the shelf inside the valley walls.

They dismounted and stood looking over the valley. Hannah put her arms about Luke and laid her head on his chest. John Lucus came up. He looked at the valley and then at his dad, and asked,

'Pa, is the war over?'

Luke pulled their son into their embrace, 'Yes, son, the war is over. We are safe now.'

Silence spread about them. Above, a hawk glided, keen eyes searching the world below. A wind rippled a field of grass below them. The peace of the valley entered into Hannah's heart and mind. They were home. Her man and son were safe. She relaxed in his arms, thinking of the days ahead for them, living and loving in their small paradise.

The publishers hope that this book has given you enjoyable reading. Large Print Books are especially designed to be as easy to see and hold as possible. If you wish a complete list of our books please ask at your local library or write directly to:

Dales Large Print Books
Magna House, Long Preston,
Skipton, North Yorkshire.
BD23 4ND

This Large Print Book for the partially sighted, who cannot read normal print, is published under the auspices of

THE ULVERSCROFT FOUNDATION